The Middle of Nowhere

Photo by Kristin Rees of Chadron, Nebraska

The Middle of Nowhere

Horror in Rural America

Edited By Jessy Marie Roberts

Chadron, Nebraska

For my husband:

Thank you for your endless patience, tireless
support and unconditional love.

LYLT,
Wifey

Table of Contents

Jameson T. Caine

The Gallery of Final Repose

"What's there to tell?" Jimmy asked. "Everyone knows the story. The guy who lived there went nuts and killed his family. The place has been abandoned ever since."

"That's not entirely true. There was a lot more to it that just that," Jay said.

Jimmy looked at Jay, then to the others before turning his eyes back to the driver. "So tell me," he said.

Jay said nothing at first, concentrating on guiding the vehicle along the winding roadway.

"It all happened when I was about six," he began, "when we lived out on Bear Valley Road. The Tauntons lived down the road from us in the next house. Of course, out there the homes are few and far in between, so even though they were our next-door neighbors, they were a good city block's distance from us. We didn't interact with them too much, but there was a family that lived on the opposite side of the road—the Petersons— whose house was halfway between ours and the Tauntons, and they passed on a lot of things to us."

Taking a sip from his soda can, he returned it to the cup holder. "Mr. Taunton worked at the mill in town, but his real passion was painting. He had a room that he'd converted into a studio, turning out portraits and landscapes and what not. He dreamt of making a living at it, but was never confident enough to display his work.

"He had a wife and two boys, though the kids were a lot older than me, like early teens or something. The family kept to themselves for the most part, but everyone knew that they had problems."

"What kind of problems?" Jimmy asked.

"Well," Jay answered, "it seems Mr. Taunton suffered from a mental illness. It could have been Bipolar disorder or Manic Depression, I don't know. Most people didn't know until it came out afterwards that he had been on medication for it. He'd refuse or forget to take his meds on occasion and when that happened, he'd end up yelling and screaming up a storm, accusing people—including his own family—of all sorts of insane shit."

"Like what?"

"Like being aliens or foreign agents or even guilty of purposely holding back his dreams of being a successful artist. That kind of thing. He'd get so loud, we'd hear it at our house. I remember thinking that it would be kind of scary having a dad that acted like that, and was glad that mine was boring and normal.

"Anyway, one week there had been a particularly loud screaming match at their house. Everything finally quieted down late that night, but nobody saw any of them for days afterwards. The kids didn't show up at school and we didn't see Mrs. Taunton working in her yard. The exception was Mr. Taunton himself. He continued to leave the house and go to his job at the mill each day."

The Camaro came around one last turn, the roadway splitting further ahead. One direction led into town while the other veered off toward the nearby farmland. Jay followed the latter course while continuing with this story. "One day about three or four days later, Taunton gets into an argument with a coworker. No one knows what it was about, but Taunton pushed the guy into one of those huge vertical saws that split logs down the middle. The poor guy was sliced in two like a ham. Taunton was subdued by the other workers and eventually, when the cops came to his house, they found everyone there dead—murdered."

"How?" Jimmy asked. In the mirror, he saw a morbid smile on Jay's face.

"That's just it, he didn't kill any two of them the same way. One of the boys he'd hung by the neck from a cross beam in the barn. The pulley system they found made it clear that he'd toyed with his son, lowering him long enough to breathe, then hoisting him back up off the floor. How long it took the poor kid to die is anyone's guess, but it wasn't quick.

"Same with the other son. That one they found tied up, drowned at the bottom of the well. They think Taunton toyed with him as well, submerging him to the point of drowning and then letting him up for a few quick gasps of air."

"That's horrible," Jimmy said.

Jay nodded. "Yeah, but the worst was what he did to his wife."

Jimmy looked at the others. Ed and Donny were nodding, obviously having heard the details before. "What happened to her?" he asked.

Jay looked at Ed. "You tell him."

Ed turned and looked at Jimmy. "He killed her with the fireplace poker."

Jimmy frowned, puzzled. "What's so terrible about that?"

"He didn't hit her over the head with it," Ed explained. "He impaled her with it, while it was red hot."

"That *is* pretty bad," Jimmy said.

Shaking his head, Ed said, "No, you still don't get it. He didn't stab her in the gut with it. He shoved it up parts of her body, if you know what I mean."

Jimmy sat confused for only a split second before realization dawned. "That's horrible!" he gasped.

"That ain't the end of the story," Donny said. "There's more."

"What?"

"When the cops searched the property and found the bodies, they also found Taunton's studio. On the wall were these detailed paintings he'd done of his family—*after* he'd killed them. The police tried to keep it all hush-hush, but word got out about it and how creepy they were."

The four sat quietly for a moment, each in their own thoughts. Outside, twilight had faded into the deep darkness of night, the moon the only source of illumination as the car followed the twisting road past fields and pastures lined with oaks, sycamores and pines. Finally, Jimmy broke the silence. "You guys are pulling my leg."

"Nope," Jay said. "It all happened. Just ask my mom the next time we're at my house. It was one of the reasons my parents decided to move into town. You wouldn't believe half the shit that goes on out here in the farmland."

"So what happened to Mr. Taunton?"

Jay shrugged. "He committed suicide in jail before he could be brought to trial. Managed to rip out his throat with a plastic fork. As for the house, no relatives ever came forward so the county put all the Tauntons' belongings into storage and tried to sell the place, but nobody has ever bought it.

"Rumors say that people have gone missing inside over the years. A few people even claimed to see the ghost of Mr. Taunton puttering around the property at night. The house has just sat empty and abandoned all this time. Speaking of which, here we are."

Jimmy looked out the window. So engrossed in the conversation, he had failed to take note of their passage through the countryside. Now he saw that they were somewhere out on Bear Valley Road, pulling up before a dilapidated house that sat a few dozen yards off the street.

The Taunton home was a two-story abode built in the style of the Victorian era. At one time it bore a light blue paint scheme, but now years of neglect had left it dulled and dirty. Loose boards and paneling had fallen to the ground, many lost amidst the weed-choked front yard. The windows sat boarded over, lending a decaying feel to the gloomy atmosphere.

Jay maneuvered the car behind some overgrown bushes and killed the engine. With the car concealed from any passing traffic, the four youths piled out. A cold wind squeezed through the trees that lined the property, bringing with it the sound of a thousand crickets, each one chirping madly into the night. Further down the isolated stretch of road, two more homes could be seen, though neither displayed any sign of habitation.

"Why are those other places empty?" Jimmy asked.

"No one wants to live near to the haunted house," Jay explained. "C'mon," he added, motioning with his hand. He approached a worn picket fence and hopped over, the others following. They made their way to the front porch, which creaked under their feet when they stepped onto it.

Ed tilted his head toward the front door. "So, there it is. Go on in," he told Jimmy.

Jimmy sized up the heavy wooden door. "I can't."

"Afraid?" Donny asked, teasing him.

"No," he said. "I can't get in because the door is locked, you moron."

"Oh," Donny said. "Then go in through a window."

"Yeah," Ed added. "Those boards should be easy to pry loose."

Jimmy turned and looked at the nearest window. Indeed, the thin planks nailed in place as cover looked rather flimsy and worn. He walked over and reached for one.

"Wait," Jay said. "Let's try a window around back, just in case anyone drives by and happens to see us. The last thing we need are the cops on our ass."

Leading the way, Jay took them around the side of the house where the weeds were even thicker. Pushing their way through, they emerged into a fenced back yard where a crumbling concrete patio provided refuge from the overgrown foliage. A barn loomed out of the darkness some fifty feet away. Its doors stood open, revealing a black maw ready to swallow anyone who ventured too near. Partway between the house and the barn, set off to the left a few yards, was an old stone well. Jay directed everyone's gaze back at the house, pointing out several large pieces of plywood that had been nailed over what had been a sliding glass door at one time.

Jay approached one section and grasping it, began to pull. "Help me, guys," he said, his teeth clenched. Ed and Donny moved to help. Within seconds the lower corner of the plywood came loose. Pulling it back and creating a small passage by which to gain entrance, Jay gestured at Jimmy. "You first. We'll be right behind."

Without a word Jimmy pulled a lighter from his jacket, lit it and then bending low, eased through the opening. "I can barely see a thing," he muttered as he disappeared into the darkness.

As soon as he had cleared the plywood, Jay shot a knowing glance to both Ed and Donny. Letting go of the board, he allowed it to fall back into place with a bang.

"What the hell?" came Jimmy's startled response from inside. "What are you guys doing?"

Ed looked at the others and held a finger to his lips. He placed his hands against the plywood and pushed. The large board was jostled when Jimmy nudged it from the other side. Both Jay and Donny, smiling, took up positions alongside Ed, helping to keep the barrier in place.

"What are you guys doing?" Jimmy called again, his voice muffled. "This isn't funny at all." He had ceased pushing and was now addressing his friends. "If you think I'm gonna get all scared in here, you can think again. I'm just fine."

Several seconds elapsed before Jimmy spoke again. "Guys?" The trio stifled their laughter as they maintained their positions.

"Okay, that's enough. Either come on in or let me out. I don't feel like standing here all night with my thumb up my…what was that?"

A long moment of silence followed. No sounds came from within, but the threesome outside did not relinquish their places.

"Guys?" came Jimmy's voice, now sounding more distant than before. "Did you guys plan this? Do you have someone in here waiting to scare me?"

Ed and Donny looked to Jay, who only shook his head. "I didn't plan anything," he whispered.

"C'mon guys!" Jimmy called, an edge of panic creeping into his voice. "Say something! There's someone in here. I can hear them moving around upstairs."

"What's he talking about?" asked Donny. "I don't hear anything."

"Ignore him," replied Ed. "He's just trying to psych us out in return. If there is somebody in there, it's probably some drunken squatter. They'll probably scare the crap out of each other."

"There's someone here!" Jimmy yelled. "They're coming down the stairs. Let me outta here. Guys? Let me out!" The plywood began to shake from Jimmy's efforts to escape.

"I think we've scared him enough," Donny said. "Let him out."

"Okay," Jay agreed. He let go of the board, but it held firmly in place, despite Jimmy's desperate pushes against it. "It's stuck. Help me move it." He pulled at the wood, but it refused to budge this time, not even when the others added their strength.

Inside, Jimmy was now screaming, abandoning all pretenses at being calm. "Let me out!" he yelled over and over, beating his fists on the plywood. "Someone's coming! Someone's coming!"

"Pull!" groaned Jay. The others were straining just as hard as he was, but the plywood board did not move so much as an inch.

Abruptly, Jimmy stopped screaming. The sudden quiet took the others by surprise and they ceased their efforts to pull the board loose. They looked at the house, wondering what was transpiring within. "Who are you?" they heard Jimmy whimper. "What do you want?"

More seconds ticked by, but no response to Jimmy's questions were forthcoming. They heard only Jimmy's voice, filled with soul-rending terror, as he screeched, "*You*! Stay away from me! *Stay away*!"

There was one final scream, long and horrible, that faded away all too slowly, like a man tumbling into a great abyss.

Then all was silent.

"He was just playing with us," Jay said. "Right?"

"Yeah," Ed said in reply. "He was probably..." He stopped and spun around, staring at the well.

"What's the matter with you?" Jay asked.

"I thought I heard water splashing."

"Maybe you did. It was probably just an animal that climbed down or fell into the well."

"Look!" Donny suddenly hissed. He pointed at the open barn doors.

"What?" asked Jay, staring into the darkness. "What is it? I don't see anything."

"Something moved. Like..."

"Like what?"

"Like something swinging back and forth inside the barn as if it was hanging from the rafters."

Jay rolled his eyes. "Are you guys and Jimmy all in this together? Cuz if you are, I don't have time for this shit." He tried the board again and this time the plywood yielded to his grasp. "C'mon," he said. "Let's go find him."

The three crawled through the opening into the darkened interior of the Taunton house. Each produced their own lighter, providing a meager source of illumination.

There was no furniture or fixtures of any kind, only empty, decaying rooms with moldy carpet, cracked paint and torn wallpaper. "Where is he?" asked Donny.

A scream pierced the still air in response, short but laced with agony and despair.

"Upstairs!" Jay shouted, bolting for the staircase. Ed and Donny were right on his heels, the three of them bounding up the steps. At the top, they dashed into the first room they saw, finding it empty. Likewise with the second. A third door revealed a bathroom. "Where the hell did he go?" Ed wondered aloud. The group piled through a fourth door.

And stopped cold.

There on the floor, in a widening pool of blood, was one of Jimmy's shoes.

"Look!" cried Donny in shock, pointing at the nearby wall. Jay turned to look, seeing for the first time the paintings hanging there.

The first showed the image of a young man hanging from a crossbeam by a rope around his elongated neck. The second featured another youth bound and submerged at the bottom of a dirty well, his eyes wide in death. In mounting horror, Jay looked at the other paintings, each one showing a person in a state of final repose, their bodies horribly brutalized in some fashion.

"Ah, new subjects to paint." The voice was so sudden, so unexpected, that Jay nearly pissed himself in surprise. Turning, he saw a man standing in the doorway, blocking any chance at egress. His throat was torn open, a jagged wound that extended nearly from ear to ear. When he spoke, his words came out in a wet gurgle. "How do you like my most recent work?" He gestured at the farthest painting.

"Oh, shit," muttered Donny, pointing at the final piece on the wall.

Jay looked closer and saw the image of a young man nailed to a ceiling, large wooden spikes impaling his arms, legs and torso.

"Look at the face," Ed said, his voice shaking.

Jay's stomach twisted when he saw that the features on the figure belonged to Jimmy. The anguished expression on that familiar face chilled him to his core.

A low moan sounded in the room.

Jay spun, seeking the source, finding only the throatless man slowly advancing upon them, a frightening smile on his face.

Then Jay looked up, and screamed at what he saw.

About the author:

Jameson T. Caine drives a tanker truck by day and calls himself a writer by night, the latter fueled by a steady diet of soda and salty snacks. He has stories appearing in the Devil's Food anthology, Sand #5, Lurid Lit, The Monsters Next Door #8, 52 Stitches, Everyday Weirdness, Flashes in the Dark and Tweet the Meat. He lives in Northern California with his wife and two dogs, where he travels many a lonesome country road as part of his job. Visit him online at www.jamesontcaine.blogspot.com/.

Kyle A. Steele

The Farm

The little boy stared out the window and cupped his hands over his eyes to shield them from the yellow light in the kitchen. "I'm not going out there," he said.

"Oh, yes you are, Stevie!" the older boy replied as he nudged his younger brother with his shoulder.

Stevie saw a fresh blanket of snow covering the ground. He looked out to where it extended into the night and became black. Shifting his weight from one foot to the other he contemplated what could be hiding in the darkness. The older boy stood behind him, arms crossed.

"Dad said you gotta go out there and get us some wood."

"Why do *I* gotta go out there?" Stevie asked. "Dad said for *one* of us to go out there and get some wood."

"'Cause I said so," his big brother replied.

"But, I don't wanna."

"I don't care what you want. You're going to go out there, and you're going to get the wood, just like Dad said."

"Why don't we just use the 'lectric heat?" Stevie asked.

The older boy glanced over his shoulder. Their father dozed on the sofa, and their mother stared at the television. "You know how mom and dad get when the bills start coming in. Just go out there and get the wood." He leaned over and lowered his voice. "You scared there might be aliens out there like on that T.V. show?" He glared down at his younger brother, moved closer and dropped his voice to a whispered. "You're scared."

"I ain't scared," Stevie argued, but the quiver in his voice told another story. He knew he was beaten. He slipped on his coat, hat, gloves and boots, picked up the canvas sling they used for carrying wood, and eased the door open. The absolute darkness struck him as hard as the frigid air that slapped against his face.

"Go on," his brother said, pushing him out the door.

Stevie stood on the small porch and watched his brother shut the door. He heard the click of the deadbolt sliding home.

"I'm not scared," he whispered, turning to stare into the darkness. The snow muffled the usual night sounds and it was completely silent.

That's good. I'll be able to hear something if it tries to sneak up on me.

He stepped off the porch into the soft snow and paused. He kicked a boot in the powdery dust.

Something could come up and pounce on me and I wouldn't hear a thing.

He scanned the yard and farm buildings. The chicken coop was quiet and his dad's tool shed was undisturbed, but he gasped when he saw the barn door standing ajar.

Is something staring back out at me?

He could not see anything through the thick dark.

I'd see the eyes glowing, wouldn't I? Maybe, if the thing were an animal or human. Aliens might have some special powers that allowed them to see in the darkness without letting their eyes shine. *And what about ghosts? Did they even have eyes?*

He shuddered, unable to look at the barn anymore, and turned away. His eyes adjusted to the blackness and he stared out into the fields that stretched beyond the farm buildings, looking for a predator, but he understood the limits of his vision. *Things could be swarming up just past where I can see, readying themselves to attack.*

He looked at the trees on the edge of the yard, the most dangerous spot. They offered a good hiding place, and they were close. *If something attacks from there it would be on me before I have a chance to get back to the house.*

Not much he could do except scan for glowing eyes. He saw none and turned to the woodpile, located under a makeshift awning his dad erected behind the tool shed. *Well, at least it's not close to the barn and whatever might be inside it.*

He took a deep breath and inhaled the crisp air tinged with the aroma of smoke from their fireplace. *Focus on that woodpile and walk fast. Load up and get back to the house.*

He started off at a brisk pace, the snow swishing under his boots the only sound he heard until a train whistle wailed in the distance.

He stopped.

Far off he heard the high-pitched yipping of coyotes, too far away to hurt him. The wind picked up and blew through the leafless trees causing the dry branches to screech against each other. *Those darn limbs could cover sounds for anything trying to sneak up on me.* He scanned the yard, but nothing had changed, and he took off again.

By the time he reached the woodpile, his heart was racing and sweat dripped down his back in spite of the cold. He loaded several split logs into the sling, taking several pauses to check over his shoulder and ensure he was still alone. *I can't let something get me while I'm loading up.*

With his task finished, he took one last look around, holding his breath so it would not interfere with listening for any noises. Satisfied, he wrestled the sling up with two hands, hoping he had filled it with enough wood to last the night, and turned to the house.

Going back was always the easiest part. He could focus on the lights in the house and see, with each step, how much closer he was to safety. The sling banged against his knees, forcing him to waddle through the snow, but he moved as fast as he could. His anxiety built with each important step.

Something could be right behind me.

He reached the porch, and let up ever so slightly, then remembered to push on. He had seen enough movies to know that many lives had been lost on those last few steps. He looked up at the window where light peeked out from around the curtain, and saw the shadow.

It moved fast, on all fours, then rose to its hind legs and hobbled out of view. Stevie stopped, dropped the sling, and watched as the shadow, back on all fours, raced across the curtains again. It was huge, with pointed ears and a long snout. A scream started, but was cut short by a meaty thud. Panicked muffled yells were followed by more of the sounds, reminding him of the noise a bag of oranges made when his mother brought them home from the store and dropped them on the kitchen counter.

A clicking sound drew Stevie's attention away from the window. The doorknob was moving just a little bit as someone or something tried to open it.

"I ain't afraid," Stevie whispered, picking up a piece of wood. But the door did not open, the lock still bolted.

Everything was silent for a moment, just before the lights went out. His brother screamed on the other side of the door, then a snarl came from somewhere in the house.

Stevie took a step back and hoisted the wood above his head, tears sliding from the corners of his eyes. He heard more screams, thuds and crashes, and then turned and ran across the yard into the darkness.

He raced across a windswept field, turning his ankles on the stubs of cornstalks left from the fall harvest. He kept going until he felt branches grabbing at his arms and legs and scratching his face. He continued until he saw, off in the distance, a light shining in the window of a small farmhouse.

Focus on the lights in the house and see, with each step, how much closer you are to safety.

About the author:

Kyle Steele lives in Atlanta, Georgia with his wife, two dogs and two kids. Kyle's day jobs have included: Army Officer, suit salesman, door-to-door window salesman, production foreman and buyer. He writes at night. His stories have been published in The Blotter, Twisted Tongue & Sinister Tales.

Jessy Marie Roberts

The Experiment

They were like no other animal he had ever studied, Dr. Alexander Bird realized after three weeks of intense observation. The University had run out of funds for Dr. Bird's research on a human growth hormone serum and had refused to allocate money for test animals. It was an easy enough problem to overcome living and working in a dilapidated farmhouse in the northeast corner of Nebraska. Field mice scratched and clawed in the walls of the ramshackle structure. All he had to do was catch them in a live trap and perform his experiments on them.

He had collected twelve that were not like the other common mice. They were small, vicious, rodent-like creatures, and they were resilient. Their epidermis was so tough and thick that regular medical instruments could not penetrate their skin. His needle tips broke when he tried to take blood samples, his scalpel could not slice off tissue samples, and none had perished.

The most notable thing about the creatures was their hunger—they had voracious, carnivorous appetites. They thrived when the doctor tossed bits of raw hamburger and poultry into their cage. He even fed them some of the mice he had collected to experiment on. The strongest male fed first, followed by the strongest female, and so on and so forth down the chain of command.

Dr. Bird was delighted with their response to his growth compound. They had grown taller, their legs lengthening and their tales thickening. The alpha male had gained six pounds in three weeks.

Dr. Bird injected a double dose of the hormone into the water bottle affixed to the creatures' cage. They eagerly drank, as if they knew it would make them stronger and smarter.

He heard a car pull up outside of the house. It would be Jennifer Armstrong, a graduate assistant assigned to him through the University of Nebraska. She was most intelligent and capable, but altogether too nosy to suit Dr. Bird's taste. She was more a spy for the University than of any real help to him.

"Dr. Bird," she said in way of greeting, her uncommonly deep voice irritating him. If he had not been told by a respected authority that Jennifer was a woman, he would have believed her to be of the opposite sex. Her hair was buzzed in the manner of a boy drafted into the military, her dark and dingy clothes too baggy and ill-fitting, adeptly hiding her actual shape from the visible eye.

Her girlfriend, Annisa, was a surprisingly attractive and pleasant girl. Dr. Bird could not figure how they were compatible, but did not ponder the subject overly much. Romantic relationships confused him, seemed an unnecessary restriction to human evolution. Science was his mistress.

He could feel he was on the verge of a major break-through with the rodent-creatures.

"Ms. Armstrong," he replied briskly, pulling a cloth over the cage that housed his special creatures. She could test the regular field mice—he would focus on the special ones.

The noise of her cellular phone's ring tone blistered Dr. Bird's ears.

Jennifer reached into the pocket of her white lab coat and put her cell phone to her ear.

"Hey, baby girl," she groaned, a perverse leer distorting her plain and mannish features.

He picked up a pile of statistics that needed to be entered into the computer. The University loved data. He did not think the powers that be understood anything they were reading, but they liked to have the paperwork in hand, making funding for his research possible. He dropped the pile of papers on Jennifer's desk, next to her computer.

She looked at him, gave him the thumbs up sign, and flipped open her laptop. The data entry would keep her busy for hours. He could study his own findings.

*   *   *

Hours later, as the sun was setting and Jennifer was printing off hard copies of data to be submitted to the University, Dr. Bird heard strange sounds coming from beneath the cloth that covered the creatures' cage.

Hurry up and leave, Dr. Bird silently willed his assistant.

"Annisa says there is a full moon tonight," she said in her husky tone.

"Indeed," Dr. Bird muttered. He hated small talk. It was the curse of small minds.

"Yes," she continued. "We're going into Omaha to a midnight showing of some horror movie she wants to see."

Who cares, he thought to himself.

"Fun," he responded.

She fished her car keys out of her lab coat pocket.

The noises from the cage grew louder, loud shrieks of pain. The cage rattled as if the creatures were throwing their bodies against the metal bars.

"What on earth?" she asked, walking toward the cage.

"Leave it be," he hollered, blocking her path.

She easily pushed him aside. At five foot eleven, she had two extra inches of height to her advantage. He did not want to guess at her weight advantage.

She pulled the cloth off of the cage and gasped.

He was shocked, too.

Some of the creatures were in the process of transformation, but others had finished morphing into tiny beings.

They looked human.

"What is going on here?" she asked, horrified.

He could not think of anything to say. They watched as the rest of the creatures finished their transformations.

He thought they were beautiful.

"I'm calling the University," Jennifer said frantically, flipping open her cell phone.

"No," he cried out, slapping the phone out of her meaty hand.

"I don't know what is going on here, but it isn't right!"

Jennifer ran toward the door. Dr. Bird stuck his foot out, tripping her. She lost her footing and cracked her head against the corner of her desk, her laptop falling to the floor with a crash.

He crouched down next to her prone, still body. Her eyes were wide open, empty and dull. A gash on her temple trickled blood. He put his fingers against her neck to check for a pulse, but did not detect anything. He felt no remorse, no sense of wrong-doing—only a primal, instinctual urge to hide what he had done so he would not be caught.

He felt something crawl across his hand that rested against Jennifer's neck. His eyes popped open. The man-creatures were on the body, feasting on the tender, newly dead flesh.

They were bipedal. There was so much food available that they were all eating hungrily, not following the usual protocol of waiting for the alpha male to be satisfied.

Dr. Bird stood the alpha male up in the palm of his hand and raised him to eye level. He was a miniature person, proportionately perfect. He counted ten fingers and ten toes.

"What are you?" Dr. Bird whispered, bringing his hand closer to his face.

"What do you think I am?" the creature responded. Dr. Bird gasped, almost dropping the being. "Yes, I can speak when I am in human form," the creature added, standing upright and proud.

"I don't know what you are," the doctor admitted, moving to sit cross-legged on the floor next to Jennifer's limp body.

"We are lycanthropes," answered the alpha male. "Werewolves, specifically."

The doctor was quiet for a couple of minutes. "Why are you so small?"

"My pack has been hunted by humans since the dawn of time. We only wanted to be left alone, to hunt animals and live apart from civilization. But humans are a vicious species and murdered us until near extinction. We are shape-shifters by nature. Through the years, during our full moon transformations, we made ourselves smaller and smaller so we could live undetected by humans, feeding on mice and other small animals. We have traveled the world aboard ships, and wound up here about one hundred years ago when this house was built. We have made a den within its walls."

Dr. Bird was fascinated. "I thought Werewolves were myths, a story told by campfires to scare children," he said in a wispy, breathless voice.

"We are much more than that," said the alpha male. "We eventually realized that while we could shape-shift smaller, we were unable to make ourselves larger again. We have been as small as when you first captured us for hundreds of years. Then you put that substance in our drinking water. Now we are growing in mass."

"That is wonderful," Dr. Bird said, his voice quivering with excitement. "This is the greatest day of my life, the culmination of my career. I have discovered a new species!"

"Please," the alpha male interjected, "please do not tell anyone of our existence until we have grown larger and stronger. Though we pose no threat to humankind, there are those amongst your species who wish us harm. They are afraid of anything different from themselves. They will slaughter us."

Dr. Bird was quiet while he thought through his options. He would increase the dosage of growth hormones to achieve quicker development, documenting the process thoroughly with pictures and quantitative data. When he revealed a full-grown man-wolf to the world, he would be the most acclaimed scientist of his time.

He outlined his plan to the alpha male, who agreed that it was a fine course of action.

***

Dr. Bird increased the dosage of the growth hormone daily. The werewolves were growing bigger

and stronger by the hour. The most interesting
development was that with the increased dosage
of the engineered serum, the creatures were able
to transform into their human form without the
full moon.

The alpha male reveled in being able to choose
between man and wolf. He had helped to dispose
of Jennifer's bones while in his wolf state,
burying them deep within the earth in different
piles. The flesh had long since been consumed by
the rest of the pack.

"You stand over six feet tall," Dr. Bird said
to the alpha male as he measured and weighed him,
diligently jotting down notes for his data.

"Yes. This is the tallest I have ever been.
I was five foot six inches tall before I willed
myself smaller. I am very pleased with your
work, Dr. Bird."

The doctor smiled. He enjoyed his conversations
with the werewolf, could confide all of his deepest
and darkest secrets without fear of judgment or
reproach. He would miss these times the most,
the intimate conversations, when he revealed his
discovery to the world.

All of the wolves had met or exceeded their
original height. Additionally, they were markedly
stronger than they had ever been. Dr. Bird was
out of the growth serum and ready to publish his
results.

"I appreciate all you have done for the pack,"
the alpha male said, holding his hand out to the
doctor.

Dr. Bird smiled and shook the wolf's hand.

The alpha male's large fist closed around the
doctor's hand painfully. The doctor's eyes
widened, looking at the alpha male with a mixture
of confusion and fear.

The werewolf snarled, his canine teeth extending into sharp points. He was able to control which features transformed into the wolf. He threw the doctor onto the floor and subdued him with a knee in the chest.

The wolf sniffed the air, growing aroused and hungry by the smell of fear. He leaned down over the doctor and licked his throat, his tongue flicking over Dr. Bird's pulsing jugular vein.

"I feel a little guilty, doctor. I wasn't exactly forthcoming with the truth about my past. You see, the humans were right to try to eliminate us. We are higher on the food chain," the alpha-male whispered, fur sprouting out on his face as the blood-lust tested his new found control over his shifting.

"But I helped you!" the doctor shouted indignantly, desperately trying to get out from beneath the powerful creature.

"That was your mistake. But I thank you. You've made us bigger, stronger, faster than we have ever been. You have created your own doom."

The doctor screamed as the wolf-man bit into his neck, tearing the flesh open. The other wolves raised their heads to the moon and howled as their leader devoured their creator.

About the author:

Jessy Marie Roberts lives in Western Nebraska with her husband, Alva, and their two dogs, Tucker and Snags. She grew up in Morgan Hill, California.

14

The summer of '79 was one of the hottest in Clark County history.

Jack's station wagon broke down on Route 41, and the three mile walk, coupled with the blistering ninety-seven degree heat, left him a sodden mess by the time he reached the nearest service station. Unfortunately, no wreckers were in commission, and he was stuck until one could be sent from down the road. *Could be tomorrow, could be Thursday*, the attendant shrugged.

With plenty of time to kill, Jack trekked over to the only other building in sight: The Lucky Lodge. The irony was not lost on him.

He gripped his heavy traveling salesman bag in one hand and pushed open the screen door with the other. The stench of smoke assailed his nostrils as he walked to the counter. He tapped the bell once and waited patiently.

No answer.

Jack leaned over the counter and caught sight of an individual watching a soap opera. "'Scuse me. I'll be needing a room."

The individual did not budge.

"I said 'scuse me," Jack called out. "Car broke down, and the heat's killing me."

The man harrumphed and got to his feet. "If yer lookin' fer relief from the heat, this ain't the place. AC busted months ago."

"Fine. Whatever," Jack replied, beyond caring. "Just get me a damned room. One with a window that opens, preferably."

"Sure. That'll be $17.50, up front."

"Rip-off," muttered Jack.

"What's that?"

"Nothing. I'll take it."

Jack exchanged his money for a room key, the number 27 clumsily etched onto the head. "Best room we got, but that ain't sayin' much. Just do yerself a favor and steer clear of ole' 14. Still hasn't been cleaned up."

He walked out of the office without a word, then disappeared down the corridor and hung a right at the intersection. 27 was the second to last door on the left. He plodded down the hall, cursing his misfortune. His latest venture barely paid enough for gas. He had no idea how he would afford to pay to fix his engine.

14 was hard to miss. The door was nondescript, but the odor wafting from beneath it was foul. Wondering what travesty was inside the room, he crouched down and peered into the keyhole.

The room was not in that bad of shape. There were a few scorch marks here and there, puzzling him. What caught his interest was a wispy feminine figure sitting in a recliner, facing the window at the opposite end of the room, curtains drawn shut. The figure was white haired and pale. There appeared to be an empty crib next to the chair. He could hear soft weeping.

Jack placed a hand on the doorknob, tempted to turn it, drawn to the figure. Everything about the scene suggested that she needed help.

Fatigue beat out curiosity. He would look further into it in the morning. He wanted nothing more than a good night's sleep.

Sleep, however, would not be restful that night. Although the window opened, there was not enough circulation to get the air flowing. That, and his dream of sweltering heat, screams, and pain kept him tossing and turning. He could not discern what the voices were calling as they sounded muted, but he had the overwhelming sensation that someone, or something, was trapped.

Unconsciousness finally claimed him in the early hours before dawn.

In the morning, Jack changed into suitcase wrinkled clothes and made his way back to the front counter.

Passing by 14, curiosity got the better of him, and he took another peek through the keyhole.

Jack saw a faint, glowing red circle with a dark center. He leaned in closer, trying to identify the source of the bright, burning color. Soft wisps tickled his eye, the color disappearing for a second, then shining again, staring at him. He jumped back, wiping his eye with the back of his hand, wondering what had brushed against him.

Jack hurried to the screen door to return the key.

"Window had a nice view, didn't it?" the clerk smirked.

"Yeah, sure did. Listen, what was up with 14? Had me a peek last night, and I could've sworn that I saw someone in there crying."

Soap Opera stared. "No kiddin'? 'Twas a fire a few months back and some lady lost herself and her baby in it. There's been a few sightings of her since, but no one's been payin' it any heed. Heat's been muddlin' their minds."

Jack found the man's answer vague and confusing, but let it go. "I didn't see much of anything

through the door a few moments ago. Just red
light. Did you change out the light bulb or
something?"

"No, I don't go in that room. You'll be
needin' to stay another night?"

"Nah. Gonna try and get a lift into the next
town. Thanks anyhow," Jack answered, reaching
for the screen door, wanting to put distance
between himself and 14.

"Ya know, there's one thing all them peepin'
toms agreed on," Soap Opera mused, looking past
Jack with a distant expression. "Her eyes."

"What do you mean?"

"How different they were from the rest of her.
Almost as if all the color in her body was sucked
right up into those glowin' red orbs."

About the author:

Christopher Jacobsmeyer is a self-styled
fantasy author dabbling in the realms of sci-
fi and horror. His tolerant wife and headstrong
daughters humor him as long as it suits their
needs. If that weren't enough, a trio of cats
keeps him in check with their whispered designs
of conquest at night.

Aaron Polson

Tommy of the Flood

Every farmer knows that the flood plain of a
river holds the darkest, most fertile soil.

The flood plain also carries risk. In a year
of heavy rain, the river will swell, crest its
banks, and swallow everything—like it swallowed
Tommy Sebelias.

***

There are three of them now, fifteen years
after the flood took Tommy. On a sodden patch
of grass in front of the house, three men stand
under the leaden sky.

"Hands in, gentleman," Derek said, poking his
scarred right palm out for the other two to
see. At thirty-three, Derek had lost most of
his hair and his once lithe frame carried a few
extra pounds around the waist. Tony and Nick
followed suit, showing the white scars each had
carved with Derek's buck knife after eighth-
grade promotion.

"Brothers," Derek said.

"Brothers," Tony muttered.

Nick hesitated a moment before adding,
"brothers."

They drank Jim Beam from the bottle in silence,
passing it around their solemn little circle.
Derek choked down a swig and brushed his shirt
sleeve across his mouth. "Shit, Nick. I can't
believe you bought Mom's old place."

"Yeah."   Nick's eyes crawled across the mud-spotted yard to the swollen ditch.   It was flood year again, and the brown murk filled around the house, leeching into the basement, the lawn, the field across the road, everywhere.   The water was cold in his bones, the smell of mud his cologne. Nick closed his eyes, trying to forget the damp smudges he saw on the bedroom floor over the past few weeks.

"Hey, dumbass."   Derek tapped Nick's arm and held out the bottle.   The amber liquid sloshed inside, and Nick's stomach tightened.

"Sorry.   Thinking."   Nick took the bottle and poured some of the contents into his mouth, closing his eyes as the whiskey burned his throat.

"Another damn flood," Tony said, his tattoos bulging from his folded arms.   He shifted weight from one foot to the other, cold in his thin t-shirt.   The rains kept the temperature down, and brought the chill from the ground, the granite cold of the grave.

Nick glanced skyward and remembered the faded grey of haunted eyes burning into him just before Tommy vanished under the water not ten feet from where they stood.   He shook his head. "Been raining for weeks. Almost non-stop. Highway ten is closed south of town again, just like…"

"You and Megan still trying to have a kid?" Derek interrupted.   They met once a year because of Tommy, because of memories that clutched to the fringes of their nightmares, but no one wanted to remember, to *really* remember.

"I suppose," Nick said with a shrug.   "Look, let's head in.   Megan's made some chili."

***

They had been the dangerous boys in high school. Derek Wochowski, with his squashed sausage face and long, ropey arms, was their de facto leader. Tony Delfino was the brawn, his nose permanently cocked to one side after he snapped it blindsiding Coach Freeman during football practice. Tony was banned from the team because of the stunt, but became a legend. Nick was always there, patient and quiet, the caretaker for their mascot, Tommy.

Tommy the Fish.

They were known for their collection of road signs, flashing construction cones, and videos that captured life from a shopping cart towed behind a truck at fifty miles an hour. They wore their scars like badges of honor.

At chronological age sixteen, Tommy Sebelias was shorter than the rest, underdeveloped and thin enough to slide through the night deposit slot at First National Bank. He was a pasty smudge of a boy, his skeleton poking out of his waxy skin. Tommy's mental age hovered around two years old. Autistic, he was always lost in his own world; most kids at school spewed hateful, venomous insults at Tommy. Not the four boys.

***

"You asleep, bub?" Megan asked as she stared at their bedroom ceiling. The room was cast in dark blue, a razorblade at midnight with the full moon sulking behind clouds.

"No." Sleep and Nick had not kept much company, not since the rains started again. Maybe he was not made for the EMT gig, either. Midnight calls to help some shriveled old bird from her bathtub never helped him sleep, never calmed his twitchy nerves. Was it Tommy he was trying to save after all these years?

"Didn't go to the Idle Hour tonight," she mumbled.

"What?"

"You didn't go out with Derek and Tony. You usually have some drinks, shoot pool."

"Oh." Nick glanced sidelong at Megan's silhouette, trying to remember her hair when it was long. Before she hacked it off after the last failed fertility treatment, Megan had the most beautiful brown hair, oaken and spun in natural curls. "I guess we're just getting too old. The bar's filled with nineteen and twenty-year-olds."

"Too old," Megan said, almost to herself.

They lay in silence for a few moments, listening to the faint tap of rain on the window.

"Why didn't the guys want to stay out here? We've got plenty of space."

Nick knew why, but the words stuck in his throat and caught like sludge in his mouth. "I dunno," he muttered. The silence in the house became a thing, took on life, almost drowning the patter on the window.

Megan rolled toward the wall. "Mmm-hmmmm. G'night."

***

Tommy had been Nick's neighbor, the kid that would always be a kid, the weird one, the freak. Derek, Tony, and Nick started hanging out in the fifth grade, back when BMX was their calling, and they spent muddy spring days hopping through the rutted rail yards down by the grain elevators.

"Nick," Tommy said one afternoon when the mud lost its luster, "let's mess with that retard next door."

"He's not retarded. He's autistic."

"Artistic, whatever. C'mon."

They took turns knocking on the Sebelias's front door. Tommy's babysitter—he always had a caretaker with him, usually a local college student—answered the door while the other two mooned Tommy. He clapped and hooted like a horny baboon and the babysitter would hurry in and calm him down.

***

The nights had been quiet until a little over a month before the reunion. Only the rising chorus of frogs and insects washed against the outside of the house with the steady pat of rain. Always a bit of an insomniac, Nick sat in his old recliner watching TV, worrying about the sleep he was not getting, when a scraping, muted sound came from the back door. Nick imagined Tommy's long, bony fingers, like overgrown insect feelers, sliding against the door. He wrenched himself from the chair, stumbled to the window, and peered outside, expecting some brazen raccoon or half-blind opossum on the back stoop.

He found muddy footprints on the mat.

The thought caught Nick around the back of his neck with long, bony fingers.

Tommy wanted out of the rain.

Nick lay wakeful after that, waiting for the sounds again, the little knocks and scrapes.

***

After a few nights, every noise became Tommy, and Nick took midnight drives to clear his head. Megan woke on occasion, her brow furrowed, reaching out for her husband. As the rains worsened, Nick contended with the devouring darkness and sludge of the country roads.

He steered toward Cedar Court, the one motel in town. It was only filled during hunting season. Derek was staying there, room 121. Nick dimmed his truck lights in the parking lot and drove past. The TV was still on, its light subdued by the curtains.

After five minutes in the parking lot, Nick stood at Derek's door. His knuckles struck the glossy, red surface. "Derek," he called, whispering. "Derek…you awake?"

The dampness crept into his bones; Tommy crept into his bones. Shadows morphed, uttering Tommy's last guttural howl. Every time Nick closed his eyes he saw Tommy sinking into the flooded ditch.

Tommy was everywhere at three in the morning during the rainy season. The rain tapped cold and steady against Nick's jacket.

He turned the knob, and, discovering the door unlocked, pushed inside to find Derek's body on the bed, his head peeled open, the wall behind him an abstract painting of blood-black streamers scribbled across the wall. The room flickered dimly with light from the TV.

"Fuck."

Nick immediately knew all the EMT training in the world could not put the dribbles of brain matter back into Derek's skull. Despite this knowledge, he rushed to the bedside and wrapped his fingers around Derek's limp wrist, desperately searching for a pulse, anything.

Suicide, the pistol announced from the floor next to the bed.

Nick's cell phone slipped from his shaking, blood-soaked hands as he dialed 911.

As he stooped to grab the phone, his eyes froze upon the wet, mud-stained prints across the motel carpet.

***

After eighth-grade promotion, the three formed a sacred union in Derek's tree house.

"Brothers," Derek said, slicing into his meaty palm.

Hesitating slightly at the sight of blood, Tony and Nick followed suit. They sealed the hallowed bond with a chug from a can of Old Style stolen from the refrigerator Derek's dad hid in their garage.

He was not allowed to be a blood brother, but Tommy had always been at the core of their group. By their freshmen year, Tommy's parents, trusting their neighbor's good nature, enlisted Nick to watch him on a few occasions, times when his regular sitters were unavailable.

It was Derek who taught Tommy how to flip off cars, and then they made excuses when a driver pulled over and barked in his face.

"He doesn't understand," Derek would say, while Nick played caretaker to the grinning Tommy, patting him down like he was out of control, a wild man.

***

A puddle of water in the rutted cemetery path pulled at Nick's peripheral vision, drawing his eyes away from Pastor Mills as he added the final sermonizing to Derek's life. Derek had not lived in town for seven years, but his folks still did. Megan squeezed Nick's arm, dragging his vision back to the black-clad throng.

"Sorry about Derek, bub," she whispered in his ear.

Nick nodded, feeling the invisible pull of the puddle, the water that saturated his world. Tommy was there, everywhere, in the stagnant water. In the glint of aluminum on Derek's casket, Tommy's eyes flickered.

"What a waste," Tony muttered under his breath. The service over, they turned—Megan, Nick, and Tony—and started toward the row of parked cars. Their shoes ground against the gravel of the drive, occasionally sucking into muddy patches where the rocks had been worn into the earth.

"You're staying with us tonight, right?" Megan asked. Short, damp curls kissed her forehead, but the brilliant green of her eyes was dim under the granite sky.

"Yeah, if that's fine with you." Tony twitched uncomfortably in his suit and shoved both hands in his pants pockets. Formal was never his style. "I want a good night's sleep before I drive home."

"Sure," Nick said. "Glad to have some company."

***

The first flood came in the spring of their sophomore year, and the whole world hushed into a grey haze. They were restless, just old enough to drive, but the world was too saturated. The Republican River crested its banks on the west and south side of town, blocking the highways.

Derek lived with his mother in a little farmhouse with a stand of apple trees, a couple of good hunting acres, and a small pond stocked with peppy little perch and a few smallmouth bass. Tommy loved fishing—watching while the others dragged the squirming, silver things from the pond.

Tommy the Fish.

They spent many soggy spring days at Derek's place. His mom left most weekends to be with Reggie, her boyfriend, in Kansas City. The farm was theirs.

"This stupid rain," Tony complained. "This stupid rain is going to wash everything away."

"Sucks," Nick muttered. His fishing gear was in the trunk, but the sky had other ideas.

Derek nodded to Tommy. "How about him? You think he wants to go fishing?"

"In this shit?" Nick waved to Derek's picture window. "He'll get pneumonia."

"You chicken all of a sudden?" Tony thumped Nick on the shoulder.

"Yeah, who used to light all those ladyfingers and laugh his ass off when they'd explode in Tomster's hand?" Derek smiled and moved to the front door.

Nick frowned. "You did, asshole."

"Oh, yeah." Derek smiled. "Hey, Tommy," Derek called in his best pied-piper voice, "you want to fish, buddy?"

Tommy nodded, his mouth hanging open.

"Out there, buddy." Derek pointed across the yard at a ditch next to his gravel drive. The ditch ran parallel to his road, and it was deep in spots: four, five, maybe six feet, connected to other fields by a series of culverts. In that water brewed a storm of chemicals and fertilizer run-off from the surrounding farms.

"Derek, c'mon," Nick sat up on the couch. "Stop screwing with him."

"Nick's gone limp." Tony dangled his hand in the air and chuckled.

Meanwhile, Tommy stumbled from the front door and waited in the rain. He stood in the downpour, grinning at the looming clouds. He looked silly, a soggy white noodle of a boy in soaked clothes.

"Go on," Derek said. "Big fish." He held up his hands.

Tommy forced his hands into two clutching claws, and staggered toward the ditch.

"Get 'em, Tomster. Jump in there!"

Tommy's eyes were as grey as the clouds.

***

There were no eyes in the bottom of Nick's beer bottle after Derek's funeral.

"What a waste," Tony said and downed the rest of his drink. "Derek was a helluva guy."

Nick shivered, still chilled to his bones, frozen from within. His mouth opened without permission. "Did he ever, you know, say anything to you?"

"What? About shooting himself?" Tony closed his eyes and shook his head. "No."

Nick tilted his bottle, watching the amber fluid slosh up the side. "No. Did he ever say anything about...Tommy."

"Oh." Tony waved to the bartender and pushed his bottle across the counter. His eyes locked onto Nick's. "I imagined I saw him the other day. No shit."

Nick drank, trying to avoid Tony's gaze.

"I imagined I saw him out in the field when Derek and I left your place."

"My place?"

Tony stared at Nick for a moment. "Crazy, right?" He laughed and shook his head. "I'm buying the next one, so drink up."

***

Just before he disappeared into the ditch, Tommy Sebelias looked at Nick, looked right at him with his faded eyes—grey as rain—and broke into a run toward the water, roaring. He could not speak, but sounds—guttural, awful things—sometimes escaped his throat. He ran straight for the ditch and disappeared with a brown splash. Nick hopped from the couch.

Derek laughed.

Tony fell down laughing.

Nick counted.

"Did you see that shit?" Derek asked, his face split in a stupid grin.

1...2...3...

"Motherfucker," Tony said, pounding the ground.

4...5...6...

"Where is he?" Nick asked.

7...8...9...

Derek's smile melted. He stepped onto the front stoop.

10...11...12...

"Where the fuck is he!"

Just like that, Tommy Sebelias was gone. Fully clothed, Nick waded in and dredged the ditch with his bare hands. Tony and Derek stood in the yard, struck dumb and pale as grubs. Soaked, covered in mud and tears, Nick called the sheriff, watching as the fire and rescue unit searched the surrounding fields, sent men into the murky culverts.

No Tommy.

The weather cleared, and the summer sun burned off the water in the fields.

They never found Tommy's body.

***

When they arrived home after Derek's funeral, the floor of Nick's bedroom was damp again. Small smudges of mud and water dribbled like footprints across the hardwood. His legs felt uneasy, his stomach churning as the pungent, murky odor of mud and grass crawled into his nostrils. Stumbling a little, he climbed into bed as quietly as possible not to rouse Megan.

She rolled toward him. "I couldn't sleep."

"Sorry."

A few moments passed. Nick tried to close his eyes, but the air became heavy. The cloying, earthy smell dissipated, but something else was in the room, choking the space between husband and wife.

"Nick...I'm pregnant."

Suddenly, he was aware of the blood throbbing in his ears.

"Pregnant?" Nick asked with wavering voice.

"Just a couple of months, maybe. I took the test yesterday...I didn't know when to tell you." Megan touched his arm under the sheet. Her fingers were fire, launching sparks through his muscles, working against the chilly dampness in his bones.

Pregnant.

He looked at his wife, trying to focus on her green eyes, but Nick saw Tommy's face in the dark, leering at him from behind Megan.

"Nick...are you crying?" She draped one arm across his chest.

Nick swallowed the tears. "Just...happy."

Megan climbed on top of him, and they made stiff, awkward love.

***

In the morning, Nick waved as Tony backed out of the driveway onto the gravel road. His car zipped away, a silver blur. Next to the road, the water in the ditch had receded some. The sun poked out of the iron clouds, the first sun Nick could remember in days, maybe weeks.

He still felt frozen.

He stepped inside and grabbed a jacket. "Megan?" he called. "I'm going for a walk. Just to the end of the section and back."

Under the peeking sun, his skin almost warmed, almost thawed. Nick listened to the morning sounds of the birds calling across the fields, and the distant sound of trucks grunting down the highway, two miles from the house.

He walked parallel to the ditch, watching his reflection blur and shimmer across surface, imagining the impossible, and remembering a thin, awkward boy who once upon a time disappeared under the milky-brown water. The world smelled of mud, a wet, fecund odor that promised new growth once the water receded.

Nick inhaled deeply, sucking clean air into his lungs—cool air ripe with moisture. *Megan's pregnant.* Turning back toward the house, he felt something stir inside of his chest, an understanding—a horrible *knowing*.

Then the sirens echoed from the highway. The frozen sludge lodged in his muscles, his veins, his whole being. Nick half-ran, half-trotted to the house. Megan met him at the kitchen door, shaking her head.

"The scanner was on...I didn't know...the call just came in."

***

Tony's silver Civic lay overturned off the shoulder of Wellman Road, the county highway leading into town. Nick knew it was Tony's before he climbed out of his truck.

"What happened?" Nick asked as he approached the makeshift barricade.

Bob Jantz, the sheriff deputy on duty, shook his head. "Sorry, Nick. It's—"

The ambulance interrupted him as it blew past, lights off with no siren.

"He was dead when we got here." Bob dropped his head.

Nick looked at the car. It was half-submerged, the cab underwater.

"Drowned." Bob patted him on the shoulder.

In a trance, Nick stumbled toward the side of the road.

"They think he swerved, like he was trying to avoid something…" Bob's voice trailed away as Nick slid down the muddy embankment. He saw the tracks. Tony *had* swerved from the highway, lost control, and rolled into the flooded field below, only a few hundred yards from where the Republican River crested its banks.

Nick's feet sank into the muck, and dirty water swirled about his waist as he waded toward the car. Sparkles of sunlight danced across the ripples spreading in his wake, but the water was cold. His bones would never thaw. He felt like drowning, like casting his body into the murky depths and letting the cool sludge slide into his throat, into his lungs, filling them until the world was black.

A dark shape writhed in the water, just ahead, only a few feet from where Nick stood. A long, lithe body.

Tommy the fish.

The water cleared and Nick could see *his* face, his eyes somehow enormous and grey despite the tainted water. Tommy smiled, his white teeth cutting into Nick's skin, a pale demon, a water-thing, more monster than ghost. His long fingers undulated under the surface like obscene tentacles. Nick pitched forward, but someone caught his arm.

"Shit, Nick. Are you trying to drown?" Bob pulled him out of the water and helped him up the embankment to his truck.

***

Nick stayed away from home the rest of the day. Idle Hour opened at noon, and he shot pool by himself while retired men played poker with the waitresses—twenty-somethings in skirts and low cut blouses. Megan called him twice, but Nick did not answer. He spent the afternoon and most of the evening at the bar, a decision brewing in his belly.

The sky cleared by the time Nick drove home, one of the first clear nights since the rains began. The house was dark with Megan in bed. He went to the kitchen, forced by the sludge that had replaced his blood, propelled by the rot in his stomach and the decision simmering there. His fingers found the handle of their chef's knife. Nick had not owned a gun for years, and the thought of smothering or strangling Megan was too much.

He could not look into her green eyes, faded or not, and squeeze the life from them.

The knife would be quicker.

Inside, the house was still—no rain tapping on the windows—as quiet as it had been in weeks.

Nick worked his way through the hallway, past the bathroom, and toward their bedroom. The muffled chirping of the night world outside was just enough to mask his soft footfalls on the hallway carpet, and the brief pats of his feet slapping against the hardwood of the bedroom.

His hand went numb.

She lay with her back to the door, curled in a fetal position, facing the window. The floor was dry—no footprints. Was Tommy gone? Would he come back? Nick circled and stood between Megan and the window, looking down at her wisps of hair and waxen face. He brought the tip of the knife to her throat.

His hands became ice.

Somewhere in his memory, the count started again.

1...2...3...

Tommy stared at him, searing his brain with grey eyes.

4...5...6...

Megan's smile, her dancing curls...

7...8...9...

Tommy vanished in the water. Gone, but not gone.

The numbers froze in his brain, and the sludge in his veins solidified as the ice from his hands spread through his body. He lurched backward. Bile burped in his throat, and he staggered against Megan's dresser, dropping the knife with a dull clatter against the floor.

Not Megan.

"Mmmm...Nick?" she called, her voice soft and uncertain. "Is that you?"

Nick's rubber hands clenched and unclenched. He fought tears.

"Nick?" Her eyes opened.

Nick dropped to his knees at Megan's bedside. "Yeah, Babe, it's me." She flinched as his cold fingers brushed her cheek.

"You're cold."

"Just got home." He pressed a damp cheek against her face. "I...I love you."

Nick thought of the baby, remembering he was the only one to ever look out for Tommy, as waterlogged tentacles chased up his spine.

About the author:

Aaron Polson currently lives and writes in Lawrence, Kansas, with his wife, two sons, and a tattooed rabbit. To pay the bills, Aaron attempts to teach high school students the difference between irony and coincidence. You can visit him on the web at www.aaronpolson.com.

Stephen D. Rogers

Hallowskreig

Seeing the group approach his house, Jeremy Fonda ran for the back door. He almost never got trick-or-treaters, his house being the only one on the hill, the only one for miles around. He almost never got company at all, except the occasional stranded motorist.

Fonda grabbed the mask from the nail and slid across the deck in his rush to get around front.

They looked older, which meant he could try to spook them before distributing the candy. At least they made the effort of wearing costumes, unlike his friends when they were teens in the city. He would not have liked giving candy to a bunch of punks who thought they deserved it just for showing up on Halloween.

Who was he fooling? He had trick-or-treaters!

Fonda crouched behind the bushes at the front corner, peered through the branches and stiffened.

The group was close enough for Fonda to recognize the helmets they wore. German, World War II. Silhouettes of weapons held at the ready or balanced against shoulders.

What the heck? Had a bus filled with re-enactors broken down? Would they let Fonda examine their equipment?

Fonda had been a World War II enthusiast since he was a kid.

He frowned. They did not strut like kids, or even march like re-enactors. They simply put one

foot in front of the other as though they had
already walked to the French coast and back.

As though they wanted to get to their
destination, but knew enough to conserve their
energy. As though they had already tasted the
vast Russian expanse.

The squad split, two holding position in the
middle, while two moved left and two moved right.
They were flanking him.

His house, anyway.

Since he was already outside, Fonda could maybe
retreat before they worked their way around him,
depending on how large a circle they made around
the property.

Fonda sensed they were not fooling around.

Whatever it was they wanted, they were not up
here hoping to score some candy bars.

He backed, careful where he placed his feet,
until he reached the rear of the house. Then
he lowered his shoulders and scurried downhill
through the underbrush as quickly as he dared.

What was he looking at here, a bunch of neo-
Nazis? Survivalists? Nuts?

What did they want from him?

Fonda did not like the idea of abandoning his
house to them, but what were his options? Even
if the guns they carried were not real, six
outnumbered one.

And the fact tonight was Halloween? Were they
members of some Satanic cult?

Motion in front of him. Fonda slid to a stop.

They could not have worked around him yet.

But who else would be coming up through the
woods?

Lots of them. An entire line of them, in
both directions for as far as Fonda could see.
Marching silently.

A shiver went up and down his spine.

They were not beating the bushes for a missing child who had wandered too far in search for more candy. They were advancing in a ragged line, advancing on a position.

As the nearest came closer, Fonda saw the rifles they carried at the ready, bayonets attached.

Fonda picked out enough details to recognize the uniforms as the type worn by World War II Russian infantry.

Just when had the Eastern Front expanded to include Eastern Nebraska, more than half a century after Berlin fell?

As the line of Russians continued to advance, Fonda scrambled back uphill as quietly as possible.

He had a better chance of slipping through six than this human wave.

But he did not want to rush, risk making too much noise. Either side could mistake him for an enemy, and he did not understand what rules were in play here.

Were they re-enactors who had been misinformed, misdirected, thinking they were on some different property, some other hill?

Were they ghosts?

Either of those things Fonda could live with, assuming he could sit back and watch the battle unfold in life-size, three-dimensional glory. That would be even better than having trick-or-treaters come to his door.

Fonda heard a series of dull *thwumps* in the distance.

A high-pitched screeching sound.

Explosions.

Close!

He dropped to the ground.

Someone was dropping mortar rounds, either the Russians to clear the path up the hill, or the Germans to disrupt the advance.

Fonda covered his head with his arms, trying to block his ears. Rounds fell all around him.

The earth danced. Dirt sprayed. Trees shattered.

The very air seemed warped by explosions that rattled his brain.

Fonda opened his mouth and screamed into the soil, which somehow lessoned the pressure he felt building inside.

From what he could remember of his study of infantry tactics, the Russians were probably still moving with small groups in short bursts.

Fonda needed to move before they caught up with him.

Would the barrage never end?

He winced as he pulled his arms from over his head. Began to crawl. While staying still seemed safer, in fact the only logical decision, Fonda figured the odds were the same.

Prone was prone.

He could be blown to bits just was easily here as farther up the hill. Here, though, the Russians were heading.

Fonda infantry-crawled through the chaos. At least he no longer had to worry about making too much noise. Nobody could hope to hear him over the deafening roar of the bombardment.

Was he still screaming?

He was not sure he wanted to know.

It was one thing to be an enthusiast, another to be concussed by explosions.

Fonda may have mistaken entertainment for the crucible of battle, but nobody could ever mistake this for a game.

The barrage lifted.

A single explosion.

And then a second.

His back muscles slowly unclenched.

In the sudden silence rose the scream of survivors as the Russians pounded up the hill.

Fonda wiggled forward, putting as much distance between him and them as possible.

A machine gun opened up, and his bladder let go before Fonda squirmed for the lowest point he could find.

He hugged the earth and breathed quick, shallow breaths to keep his inflated lungs from increasing his silhouette.

The mortar rounds had been real. There was no reason to believe the bullets were any less deadly.

The grenades. The bayonets. The fingers tearing at his throat.

Fonda coughed out dirt and dryness, tried to spit, but failed.

A second machine gun opened up.

The weapon was close enough he could tell the fire was being directed downhill.

Anything that kept the Russians from reaching him was good, so long as it did not kill him in the process.

He needed to get through the German lines. Needed to get to the road on the other side of the hill and safety.

Fonda scurried from suggested concealment to suggested concealment.

How near was he to his house? Hard to tell when he was staring at the ground. But raise his head to look and he just might be decapitated.

Move forward, upward. Just keeping moving.

The Germans would be looking past him to the line of Russians.

Until they closed the distance.

When Fonda would be shot as a scout by the Germans or overrun by the Russians, a distinction that made no difference.

Fonda paused behind a tree to catch his breath. Finally, cover that mattered, even if only from one direction.

Rifles opened up.

Were they aimed at targets or ghosts?

The trunk splintered.

Fonda snaked his way uphill, his mouth made bitter by a metallic taste.

Fear? Could he still feel fear?

He felt so numbed he doubted he would feel the bullets that shredded him.

Shouts behind him. Words he did not understand. Orders?

Deep cracking sounds as grenades exploded.

More dirt flew. Shrapnel.

Screams.

Fonda reached a crest, the ground leveling out.

He saw out of the corner of his eye a light to his left. His house? Would the Germans have left the lights on, a beacon calling the Russians to their death?

It made sense to pull them forward rather than give them time to think. The Russians could too easily encircle the hill and then overwhelm the few defenders, trapping him here, as well.

More weapons fired. The range must be closing.

Fonda skirted land he knew.

He reached the top of the hill.

Had he passed through the Germans?

Were now both sides behind him?

What difference did it make? A Russian bullet would travel through the front lines to hit a man fleeing in the rear.

Fonda continued to scrabble through the darkness.

But to where?

Scrambling for relative safety.

His hands touched something cold.

Metal.

Fonda wrapped his fingers around the tent stake.

If he ran into the enemy, he just might owe his life to someone who trespassed on his land.

Fonda continued.

Behind him, the Germans and Russians continued to shoot at each other.

Perhaps he was wrong to be cautious.

The Germans might give ground, execute a fighting withdrawal.

Fonda might still be consumed by the front lines, might still be overrun as he crawled.

And then, if both sides somehow missed him, a counterattack by the Germans could engulf him once again.

Shouts. Screams. Gunfire.

Fonda felt the earth shift and then he was moving downhill.

He stopped and risked a look forward, then back, scanning his surroundings in a slow circle.

There was the road, off to his right. He should move parallel until he reached the highway.

Any plan was better than none.

Fonda stood.

Waited.

Began breathing again.

Moved forward downhill.

The sounds of battle grew less distinct.

He might survive this yet.

Fonda brushed off dirt. Leaves. Twigs.

Whatever happened to the mask he grabbed as he had gone out the back door to meet his trick-or-treaters?

He picked up speed until he almost galloped, trusting that after what he just survived that he would not twist his ankle on a root.

Fonda saw something up ahead.

Slid to a stop.

Listened.

A vehicle. There was a jeep parked at the side of the road. Had the Germans driven this far before marching to their position? Had they left behind a guard?

Fonda could cut away from the jeep, but his legs chose this moment to react, to quiver and ache and threaten to let him crumble to the ground.

He wanted that vehicle. He wanted the keys to be inside and the gas tank to be full. He wanted to sit on a cushioned seat and drive away.

His desires overcame his caution, and Fonda continued towards the jeep, pausing every so often to listen. To scan a three-sixty.

He heard mechanical sounds as he drew closer. Saw the jeep jerk, as if someone was cranking down the jack after changing a tire.

As soon as he reached pavement, Fonda picked up the pace.

He ran around the front of the vehicle as someone rose.

Fonda raised his arm and brought the metal stake down again and again.

Crouched and then knelt to continue bringing it down.

Hearing the screams even after the body had long stopped moving.

Realizing the screams were his own.

This was no German, no. No Russian either.

Fonda continued to scream, determined to drown out the sounds of a battle he no longer heard.

About the author:

Over five hundred of Stephen's stories and
poems have appeared in more than two hundred
publications. His website, www.stephendrogers.
com, includes a list of new and upcoming titles
as well as other timely information.

Anca L. Szilágyi

Hail

They had been driving down a country road when the hail began. The trees were dark from dampness, tall and naked in the gray December light, their wooden fingers reaching up, and goading the sky. They came first in little icy droplets. Mr. Smith turned the windshield wipers on low, sweeping slow, back and forth, as they went up and down the gentle hills.

"A flirty bit of ice here and there," Mr. Smith said.

"I think it's pretty," Mrs. Smith responded.

The couple stopped at a roadside diner for the shepherd's pie special. They ate in silence and watched the icy rain shimmy down. The waitress cleared their empty plates, and Mr. Smith brushed crumbs out of his moustache.

"Perhaps we should move on before it gets worse," Mrs. Smith speculated, reaching for her large, floral hat.

"Perhaps," mused Mr. Smith.

As they paid their bill, Mrs. Smith reached over, her fingers like pincers, and snatched out one vagrant crumb clinging to his bristly lip. They ran out to their car in the empty lot, the sky spitting small half-pebbles of ice. Mr. Smith started up the engine, and they eased back onto the road.

"It's rather heavy, isn't it," declared Mrs. Smith.

"Rather," replied her husband, leaning over the wheel and squinting.

"Only two more miles to the resort!"

This declaration seemed to challenge the weather. Instead of half-pebbles, the sky hurled marbles.

"Oh dear," sighed Mrs. Smith under her breath. A lonely house stood at a bend in the road, dark and not particularly inviting. The Smiths peered at it, hoping signs of life would emerge.

"Perhaps we should see if anyone is there and wait for the weather to let up. I don't like driving in this hail," Mrs. Smith suggested.

"It's not so bad," her husband replied, hunched further over the steering wheel, his nose twitching with concentration.

At this moment, the weather became particularly spiteful. Marbles turned into golf balls, clunking down on their car in a syncopated rhythm. The golf balls, far less charming than flirty flecks, lost further charm when accompanied by baseballs.

"Let's stop at the house," said Mrs. Smith.

Mr. Smith sighed through his nose. "Yes, all right."

He pulled into the driveway. A basketball of solid ice hit the roof of their car. They looked up at the dent and listened to the faint creaking noise.

"Quickly now," warned Mr. Smith.

"Yes, quickly."

They ran out of the car and to the front door of the isolated home, gave a requisite knock, and then barged in.

The house was empty, save one or two pieces of furniture draped in dusty cloth. Mr. Smith tried the light, but it did not work. Mrs. Smith shuddered. There was nothing to do but wait for the hail to stop.

"I guess no one lives here," she said.

"I guess so."

"Let's see if there's any tea in the kitchen."

"All right," said Mr. Smith.

They went to the kitchen, their footsteps muffled by the cacophony of hailstones pummeling the roof. The kitchen had a sun porch, and the glass was punctured in several places. Wind howled through the jagged holes.

"How dreadful," said Mrs. Smith.

"Quite."

There was no stove to speak of, no Fridgedaire, nor a sink. It was hardly a kitchen. They stared through the glass at the woodlands beyond. Boulders of ice dropped from the clouds, breaking through branches and rolling down the gentle hills.

They hurried away from the sun porch, and found some blankets in a room upstairs, piled in a corner. They shook out the dust and took them back to the center room on the first floor.

"Might as well have a seat while we wait," said Mr. Smith.

"Might as well," shrugged his wife.

They knelt on the floor in the dark house and huddled together, shivering, goose bump to goose bump. They heard the boulders splintering the roof, the lighter ones rolling down and smashing to the crispy, crunchy ground, mixing with the shattered glass of the sun porch.

And they waited.

But it never stopped.

About the author:

Anca L. Szilágyi's fiction has appeared in the *Massachusetts Review*, *Western Humanities Review*, and *Antigonish Review*, among other publications. She has previously edited the journal *Scrivener Creative Review* and the webzine *55 Words*. This fall she will begin at the MFA program at University of Washington-Seattle.

Alva J. Roberts

The Plant

Blood ran in rivers through thin channels in the dusty, dry, earth. Billy groped his way forward, his hand clutching his stomach, holding in his intestines. Chunks of flesh and pieces of his blue security uniform left a trail back into the construction site.

It was behind him, it was still coming for him.

The promise of a radio and safety of his pick-up truck kept him moving forward. He could see the rusty silver Ford. He just needed a few minutes.

Pain lanced through his body as he felt something sharp rip into his back and thrust all the way through his body, erupting from his abdomen. His hands groped across his wounded stomach, feeling the thick shaft piercing his body. His eyes rolled back in his head as he was lifted into the air.

He tried to scream, but all that escaped was a choked, blood-filled gurgle.

***

"Where the hell is Billy?" David asked, adjusting his clip-on tie.

"I haven't seen him," Tara answered without looking up from her magazine.

David hated his new position as supervisor.
Everything was so much easier when someone else
was in charge. Tara never stopped reading her
magazines, and Billy was always sneaking off to
smoke pot behind the rock piles.

They were just lucky that someone from corporate
never stopped by during the night shift. If they
did, all three of them would be looking for new
jobs.

David liked working as night shift security
at the construction site. He was contributing to
the new plant, and the hundreds of jobs it was
bringing to their rural community, without ever
getting his hands dirty. Plus, he rarely had
to do much of anything besides walk around the
cleared fields to make sure no kids were out there
getting drunk.

"Put down your stupid magazine and go find him.
We both know he's out by the rock piles," David
said, putting as much command in his voice as he
thought he could get away with. Tara had been
in his high school class, and he knew she would
be just as likely to tell him to go to Hell as
follow his orders.

"Yes sir, big boss man, sir. I'll get right on
that." Tara flipped a page in her magazine.

"Now!" David shouted, ripping the magazine
from her hands. "Take a radio and leave it on.
I'm going to be in touch with you. If I think
you've been smoking pot with Billy, you're both
fired. I'm fed up with all of this."

"Jesus. Lay off the caffeine. I'll go check
on Billy."

David scooped up the walkie-talkie and strode
over to the big chair near the security monitor.
Finally, she listened to him. He was going to
mark the day in his calendar.

The chair let out a soft hiss as he let his large frame settle into the faux leather. Three of the five monitors showed static. *Par for the course.* Everything around the security office was breaking, and no one wanted to spend a dime more than necessary on an ethanol plant that may never get built. Construction had stopped a month ago, just after they cleared the farmland.

"Oh my God! David, get out here!" Tara's voice screeched through the worn speaker.

"What's wrong? Did Billy drop his bong?"

"Shut up! Get out here! By the parking lot!"

David rushed to the door, grabbing a flash light on his way. He had never heard Tara use that tone of voice. Worry began to creep into his mind. He hoped Billy had not gotten hurt.

The parking lot was only a hundred paces or so from the office. The full moon shone bright in the sky, illuminating the construction site and the vast endless plains that surrounded them.

It was twenty miles into town.

David could see Tara standing with her arms wrapped protectively around her chest. His thumb flicked on the flashlight as he walked toward her.

"What is it?"

Tara did not say a word, she just pointed. A few feet from where she stood there was a huge puddle of blood. Tiny chunks of flesh and hair floated in the crimson liquid.

A cool breeze wafted past David's face, bringing the pungent smell of decaying corn to his nostrils. When they cleared the farmland, they left the fields to rot.

"We'll have to call the cops. Somebody must have been Poaching, and field dressed a deer out here," David said, his mind jumping to the only conclusion he could think of.

"This isn't some deer. Those are pieces of Billy's uniform."

"That little degenerate is playing a trick on us. Billy! Get your stoned butt out here! This isn't funny!" David shouted.

The shadows that lay across the ruined farm grew more ominous.

"He wouldn't go this far for a prank. He's too lazy for that," Tara said. "Hey, shine the light down here."

David did as she asked, moving the beam of light over the pool of blood. She leaned over, picking up something.

"This isn't a trick. There's no way he'd do this to his stash," Tara said, holding up a plastic lunch baggy dripping with scarlet fluid.

"Jesus. Get inside."

David ran to the door of the small mobile home office, fear churning in his gut. He did not even notice if Tara was behind him as he ran through the door, to the phone.

It would take the sheriff a good twenty minutes to get out to the site, and David wanted to get him started as fast as possible.

The phone was dead.

"What was that? Just leaving me out there? You're such a jerk!"

He could see the vein in Tara's temple throbbing, and he knew what that meant. But he did not have time for one of her angry outbursts.

"The phone's dead. I'm getting the hell out of here. They can fire me if they want," David said, interrupting her tirade before it began. Tara nodded. For the first time in the twenty years he had known her, she was speechless.

He rushed to the door, stopping to pick up Billy's baseball bat. Billy always said they would need it one day.

David could not believe that the paranoid teenager's ramblings had been right.

***

David sprinted to his car, not caring if he looked like a coward in front of Tara. He stopped caring what she thought of him ten years ago, when they were sophomores in high school, and she gave him a wedgie on prom night.

Cloud cover was moving in, blocking out the moon. The light grew dim and unsteady. David heard something rustling in the fields near the parking lot, just a few feet from where he stood.

He pulled the bat back, ready to smash whatever it was. His breath quickened and he felt his hands start to shake as adrenaline raced through him.

Tara cut through the darkness with the beam of a flashlight, illuminating a small black and white creature.

"Just a skunk," David said, shaking his head, laughing at his own reaction.

Tendrils of mist squirmed forward, from nowhere. Within seconds, the entire area was shrouded in a thick fog.

"What is that?" David shouted.

Ominous green eyes glowed in the darkness.

Something thick and slithering lashed out, knocking Tara to the dusty, dry soil. Her flashlight fell to the ground, the beam striking her attacker.

David went numb.

It was not human.

Its hunched, deformed body stood over ten feet' tall. It was the color of dried grass with black patches of dried blood. Strange scraps of pink

material hung over its body. When it stepped
closer, David realized the skin of Billy's face
was pulled tight across the monstrosity's head.
Withered vines, still showing some green, sprouted
from the beast's back.

Tara screamed, kicking at the vine that
encircled her leg. Another of the vines raised
high into the air above her, a sharp spear-like
object at the end of the vine ready to stab down
into Tara's tender flesh.

"Leave her alone!" David screamed, running
forward.

David hit the creature in the torso with his
bat with all the strength he could muster. There
was a hollow, squelching noise and a maddened
scream of rage.

A putrid, rotting smell filled the air.

David swung the bat again, striking the
creature's head. It stepped back, its vine-like
arms swinging toward David.

David flew through the air, landing hard on his
back. He made a choked gasping sound, the wind
knocked out of him. His hand reached around,
searching for the bat.

Pain shot through his ankle as a tentacle
wrapped around it, crushing his small bones and
pulling him closer to the monster. The spear-
like object raised over his head again, poised
to stab.

David's heart pounded as waves of nauseous
fear poured over him.

"Screw you!" Tara screamed, the bat in her
white knuckled hands.

The bat smashed into the creatures back,
forcing it to stumble forward. As it passed,
David saw that that the 'spears' were corncobs.
The whole hideous thing was made of rotting corn.

David pulled himself across the dirt, away from the corn fiend. He picked up a rock and threw the projectile at the monster in impudent rage, unable to stand. He did not know if he wanted to run or try to help Tara, but could not do either.

Tara's blood sprayed through the air as the vicious spikes of corn tore through her body. The bat dropped from her numb fingers. David watched her corpse fall, as if in slow motion.

There was a tearing sound as the multitude of tentacles shredded her body into pieces. Patches of fresh pink skin were added to the monster's bloody frame.

David forced himself to his feet, wobbling on the broken ankle, ignoring the pain. He hobbled forward, trying to escape the repugnant, fetid stink, and the blood. He managed three steps before his mangled ankle gave out, unable to hold his weight.

Razor sharp corn spikes grazed his face, scratching at his cheeks. Then pain, horrible, excruciating pain, encompassed the remainder of his existence.

***

"I can't believe the corn would grow back like this," a man in a black business suit said, wandering through the tall rows of corn that covered the whole construction site.

A group of men followed him through the field. They stopped in front of a scarecrow made of strange pink leather. Some perverse farmer had fashioned three faces in the material.

"Yes, sir. It seems odd. Maybe somebody replanted after the security team quit," one of his lackeys replied.

"Strange how they all quit at once, with no notice," a different lackey added.

"Have Henderson put the land back on the market. The people around here are unreliable. And for God sakes, someone tear down that scarecrow," the business man replied, heading for his limo.

Malevolent green eyes watched, for the moment sated

About the author:

Alva J. Roberts lives in a small town in Western Nebraska with his wife and two dogs. When he is not writing, he works as a librarian at the public library.

Christopher Fulbright

Death Depot

The Greyhound bus trundled through the dead of night over an Iowa backroad with washboards like the ribs of a dead man's chest. The coach shuddered, stirring the smells of unwashed bodies that swayed in the rows in front of him. Jay tried to stay awake by reading a paperback, but he could not concentrate. He set the book aside and watched the miles of undulating black fields.

A streak of light flashed across the sky.

He rubbed his eyes, then opened them again just in time to see another burst, like that of an impact, very close to the town of Draper.

No way. I'm seeing things. I need some rest. His eyes closed as he finished his thought.

***

He awoke when the bus came to a stop at the bus depot in Draper. The smells of the bus had gotten into the back of his throat and gone bad. He swished and swallowed, wishing for a place to brush his teeth.

It was early morning, still on the dark side of twilight, and only a few passengers remained on the bus. The door opened and the driver staggered out. Jay did not wait for the others to get up and move. Instead, he made his way, with cramped legs, for the front door to the depot. His fiancée, Cindy, was driving into town to meet him at 4:00 a.m.

He had to find a clock.

The depot was slightly bigger than a truck stop, on the corner of two dirt roads to nowhere. One road stretched to the midnight horizon, lined on each side by stalks of corn nearing harvest, looking like fur swaying in the manure-scented breeze.

The other road was bone-white, and bathed in moonlight. It stretched toward Draper, the lights of the town like stars on black forested hills. He took a deep breath of night air and went through the depot's dusty glass door.

The interior of the depot was cool; the air conditioning made it feel like a cave. It was practically deserted. One man slept on a bench just outside the ticket counter, and a woman with deep-set eyes tiredly wiped an already clean countertop in the cafe. A young man stood near one of the old payphones, the receiver in his hand, staring at the wall.

It smells odd in here.

The faint scent of old popcorn mingled with a hint of some unidentifiable chemical that Jay could not place. He shifted his duffle bag higher onto his shoulder and limped toward the bathroom. His legs were stiff, and it was hard to walk and keep his balance. Even the joints of his elbows felt arthritic.

I was in that bus too damn long.

Jay entered the bathroom and went to the sink, running cool water from the faucet and into his hands, and then splashing it over his face. His countenance in the grimy mirror startled him. His reflection, beneath the fingerprints and soap-spotted glass, was drawn and gaunt, showing bloodshot eyes in bruised sockets.

In one of the stalls to his right, Jay heard the shuffling of shoes on dirty concrete. He turned toward the sound, surprised to find that someone else was in the bathroom with him.

A pool of blood flowed from beneath the stall partition. Before Jay could comprehend what he was seeing, a business-suited man with sallow features and shocked, sunken eyes emerged in a lurching gait from the stall. His face and the front of his white dress shirt were covered with gore. In one hand, he held a mass of torn flesh.

Jay's breath caught in his lungs. He stepped back and spotted a corpse that lay half-eaten in the stall. Realization dawned on him as the cannibalistic businessman groaned and looked up with vague, hungry recognition. Jay spun quickly and, gasping for breath, his heart pounding, forced his way out of the bathroom door.

As soon as he emerged from the bathroom, he spotted the clock across the main room of the depot above the ticket booth. It read 4:02.

Please, Cindy, for once be on time!

The few others in the depot turned toward him as he stumbled for the front door of the depot and out into the pre-dawn twilight. Headlights pierced the gloom in the distance, headed toward the depot.

Cindy's car came into view just as Jay turned to see a blank-faced teenager with a burned-down cigarette in his hand stumbling for the door.

Cindy pulled up in front of the depot, tires snapping over gravel. She barely had time to roll down the window and say hello before Jay hurled himself around the front of the car, threw his bag into the back seat, and slammed the door. His stomach churned with a strange mixture of hunger and sickness, but he just wanted away from this place. They could call the police later.

"Jay! My god, what's gotten into you? You act like…"

"Just get us out of here, Cindy," he croaked. His throat was not working right.

"Okay." She stepped on the gas and left a rooster tail of gravel in their wake.

Down the road a ways, she slowed down and said, "Jay, are you going to tell me what happened? Did you have a bad trip?"

The car radio droned beneath her voice, just barely loud enough to be heard. A news reporter talked about an unidentified flying object that fell from the skies and landed in a cornfield in Draper. Calls were pouring in. The town had gone mad.

"Jay?"

Cindy placed her hand on Jay's knee. He looked at it for a moment, trying to figure out why it might be there, as if it absolutely did not belong. He reached down and took it in his own. He tightened his fingers around her wrist.

"Oww, Jay. You're hurting me…that's too tight…"

The hunger was stronger now, the craving too powerful to deny. He pulled her across the seat, drew the supple flesh of her forearm to his mouth, and bit deep.

Cindy screamed. Blood gushed, warm and satisfying, into Jay's mouth.

The car swerved. She lost control as she tried to fight him off. The vehicle careened headlong toward an oncoming semi-truck. Its horn blared.

He took another bite.

About the author:

Christopher Fulbright has been writing stories for as long as he can remember, with about sixty publication credits to his name, including stories, novellas, a collection, and one novel. He lives in Texas with his wife and two children, and dwells on the web at http://www.christopherfulbright.com

Jacob Henry Orloff

Crop Circles

The crop circles are talking to me. I know my family thinks I'm mad, that's why the mail has stopped coming. I fancy this will be my last journal entry before I ascend into the clouds with the ancient ghosts of the field. It is only now I realize why this farm in Kansas was so cheap! At first, the crop circles seemed like the pranks of some bored adolescents, but they are unlike anything I've ever seen! Too intricate for rope and wood planks! If only I had fled when the first circles came...but it's too late now. I am a part of them...the ones who truly shape the crops...and they are taking me tonight...

***

The dogs barked incessantly in the fields in the early morning hours of a cloudy mid-October day. Henry Jacobs, columnist for the local gazette, was perturbed. It was Saturday, his only day off of work, and his two hounds howling stirred him from a pleasant slumber.

Opening one glazed and groggy eye, he glanced over at the digital clock on his bedside table. 7:25 flashed in neon green. With a groan, he slipped out from under the warm covers, threw on some clothes, and hobbled down the steps, rubbing his eyes along the way.

The dogs still barked. No time for coffee,

this must be important. The screen door opened with a creak and snapped shut with a clap as Henry hopped down the porch steps and strode across the dew-strewn lawn. His height allowed him to see just above the tops of the corn stalks, so when he neared the edge of the field he immediately spotted open space that should not be there. Baffled, he parted the corn and slipped into the homegrown jungle.

Leaves brushed against his shoulders and chest, leaving wet streaks, while muddy soil clung to his shoes. The barking grew closer as he made his way deeper into the field until he stepped into a wide crop circle. The two hounds reared their heads, baring their teeth, then closed their mouths, panting, as they recognized their master.

A dozen dead birds lined the circle in no particular order.

He returned to the house, the dogs at his heels, and went around back to the shed. Glancing around a bit at the dusty shelving, he picked up an old pair of binoculars and stuffed them into his pocket. Then, gripping onto the rusted ladder, he dragged it outside and leaned it up against the short end of his home. He had been on the roof for re-shingling several months earlier, and he was accustomed to the height. Scrambling over the peak, he crouched down, yanked the binoculars out of his pocket, and placed them to his eyes.

There were three circles; one large circle with the scattered birds centered between two smaller ones equidistant from each other.

"Weird," he whispered.

Climbing down, he went inside and snagged the phone off the hook to make a call.

"Yeah, Sheriff? This is Henry. Henry Jacobs…
you won't believe what I have out here at the
farm…you got a few minutes to kill? You should
bring a vet, too. Why? You'll see…just get here
as soon as possible."

* * *

Nearly half an hour passed before Sheriff
McAlister rolled into the driveway. Henry had
enough time to eat a small breakfast and feed
some of the livestock by his arrival. McAlister
had a passenger, Doctor Riley. Stepping off the
porch, Henry approached the two as they came out
of the police car.

"Sheriff…Doc…" he said, shaking their hands and
smiling. "Thanks for coming by on short notice."

Henry led them into the field, first to the
center circle and then to the two outer ones.

"Well…there doesn't appear to be any physical
reason why the birds are dead…no open wounds…
no blood…nothing," began Riley. "I'll have to
take some in as specimens to do some further
examination…maybe it is some type of bacteria or
avian virus…but as far as I can tell, their wings
should still be flapping…"

The sheriff paced around the circle, examining
it inch by inch.

"I've seen crop circles before…pranks by local
teens…these seem like a simple pattern, really,
compared to some of the other ones I've seen,"
said the sheriff. "Although, I don't see any
footprints other than our own…and the circles
are quite symmetrical…I don't know, Henry. I'll
go ask the Smith twins about it. They're always
up to no good. And the Doc will get back to you
with what he finds, right, Doc?"

Riley nodded as he took a pair of tongs and picked up several of the birds, placing them in separate bags.

Henry offered them both a cup of coffee. After they stood around slurping for a bit, the Sheriff and Doctor took their leave and Henry went about his business for the remainder of the day.

* * *

Hey, Mom and Pop,

It's been awhile since I've written you. Working at the Gazette and tending to the farm out here has kept me busy. You were right! Moving out of the city and into rural Kansas was exactly what I needed. The open air, the smell of the farm… ah! It is so perfect out here. I hope you can find time to come visit your only son!

In any case, something most peculiar happened today. I awoke this morning to the barking of my dogs and found several crop circles that flattened out the corn stalks. What's more bizarre about it was the fact that nearly a dozen birds were scattered about—dead birds. The local vet is having a look at them and he should be getting back to me within the week.

Love always,
Henry

* * *

Henry put the hounds in the kennel that night for fear they contracted a disease from the dead birds. The wind blew hard, and the rustling of the crops made an ominous raucous as he strode from the barn to his house. The television displayed mostly static, which was common when a big storm was rolling in. Tired, he turned in early, and fell asleep to the swaying stalks and the occasional droplets of rain that splattered against his bedroom window.

The crack of thunder awoke him. He had always been a light sleeper. It was still pitch dark, and the clock read 3:00. He rolled over, and before he closed his eyes to fall asleep again, he glimpsed a glow coming from the outside.

He sprung to his feet and moved to the window. Out in the fields were seven bobbing bluish-tinted lights.

Flashlights!

Strapping his shoes to his feet, Henry dug into his closet for his shotgun and a fistful of shells. He jumped down the stairs and out into the lawn, leaping across his yard and diving head first into the crops, determined to catch the culprits in the act.

The lights were gone by the time he blitzed his way to the large circle. *Maybe they had heard him coming? Maybe they turned off their flashlights and are hiding nearby?* He scanned through and around the outer perimeter before giving up on pursuit.

Maybe it was just a dream.

He walked to his house, climbed into bed, and returned to sleep.

***

The next morning he awoke to his alarm and went outside to scan the circles for any footprints besides his own, the sheriff's and Doctor Riley's.

Nothing.

Work at the gazette was hectic, but all the while Henry's mind was distracted with thoughts of the crop circles. More had appeared during the course of the night. Now there were four circles, all connected by bizarre zigzagging patterns, and dotted with several minor circles whose circumference was no larger than six or seven feet.

He had seen something in the field.

After work he went through his normal routine at the farm and sat for a brief while on his porch to watch the golden sunset and write in his journal.

***

Things are progressing painfully slow at the gazette. Nothing ever really happens here, except on my farm. Those crop circles seem to keep expanding in design. I saw lights out in the field last night and I tried catching up to whoever it was, but they managed to evade me. Honestly, I don't feel like reporting this in the news; conflict of interest. And I really would prefer not to be the joke of the town if it is the Smith twins behind it with the aid of some other hooligans. While I was at work, two more circles popped out, making the total of large circles six. Several minor augments such as zigzags, arcing lines, and minor circles have been added too. This hoax is starting to lose its edge...if indeed it is a hoax. What am I saying? Of course it is! Henry...get yourself together. You're better now...you don't believe in such nonsense anymore...that's why they took you off of the pills, remember? That's why you moved

*out here into the country…to get away.   The open
space is healthy for you…that's what they said,
remember?*

***

The week slowly melted away with each new day
bringing more intricate designs to the crops.
Every night Henry sat and watched.   The lights
came, he gave chase, and he would lose them—whoever
they were.   A call for Henry at the gazette's
office broke the monotony Friday afternoon.

"Hey, it's Doctor Riley.   How are you doing?
Good to hear.   Listen, I got those test results
back.   I screened them for everything…Bird Flu,
Fowl Cholera, E. Coli, Salmonella…nothing, Henry.
Not a single thing.   No virus, no bacteria.   It's
almost as if a flock of birds just dropped dead.
Sorry I can't be much more help.   I'll let you
know if anything else comes up.   Have a good
one."

***

Mom and Pop,

I got your letter.

*There are new developments with the crop
circles. The pattern is continuing to grow and
spiral out through the whole field. I've asked
the Sheriff and the Doctor to keep it under
wraps…I don't want townies coming out here to
take pictures.   I did snap a few photographs
myself that I'm including with this letter.
These weird lights keep coming out every single
night!   I chase them, but they always manage to*

evade me. I think it may be the Smith twins and some of their friends. Who knows? I'll just be glad when the winter comes.

Luckily, I can support myself with the money from the gazette and not have to worry so much about how much the harvest will bring in. And, in truth, the pattern is quite beautiful to look at, especially at sunset.

The vet called me back and filled me in on the tests he had run. Nothing. Absolutely nothing. No reason whatsoever why those birds were dead. No poison, no disease, nothing…it's as if their hearts just fluttered and stopped. Weird.

I've been doing great without my medication, actually, and thanks for asking. Please wish Eileen a happy birthday. I'm sticking a ten dollar bill into the envelope as well, so please make sure it gets to her.

Love,
Henry.

***

"It's not the Smith twins," the phone call with the sheriff began. "They both have an alibi that I was able to confirm, killing brain cells at the local bar. I don't know Henry, it sure is weird. Maybe it's some kids from the next town over. You sure you haven't made any enemies lately? Hmm. Weird. Just plain weird. I don't know what else to do…"
A few minutes of idle conversation prolonged the phone call until Henry finally said goodbye and clicked the receiver. It was Saturday again,

two weeks had passed since the circles first appeared, and Henry was obsessed. Nightly he wrote in his journal, chased the lights, and become increasingly despondent. He hardly slept, showered, or ate—and it showed. His work became sloppy at the gazette and his boss told him to come back when he cleaned up. The ladder became permanently affixed to the side of the house and each evening Henry sat at the roof's peak and sketched out the new designs and patterns.

***

You see...as I've sketched below here in this diagram...the crop circles seem to be mapping out some sort of pattern of the stars...some sort of alignment I guess. Mom and pop phoned over to me to make sure I was doing alright. They were worried because I sent them five letters in the past week. It's just there are so many new developments in the designs. I couldn't fit all of the pictures in an envelope, so I just started mailing small packages. I'm not obsessed. I'm not obsessed. I'm really not. I told them I'm not. If they had such designs in their backyard, I'm sure they too would be a bit preoccupied! I'm going to try to camp out in the field tonight to catch whoever is doing this...not because I want to press charges or anything, but because I'm curious. I'm curious what this all means.

***

That night the man the world knew as Henry Jacobs disappeared, and a new apparition appeared out of the crops. It had the same name and form, but was different in demeanor and personality. He spoke in a similar tone, an octave or two deeper, and now the dogs loathed him. They would not go near him, nor would they eat any food he put out for them. Henry Jacobs was different. A stranger. Work resumed at the office and the crop circles ceased. He ate, slept, and showered regularly. To everyone on the outside looking in, he was the healthy man they had known two weeks prior.

Gradually, the months slipped by into the winter. The sheriff had stopped by for a visit and was surprised to find that the crops had not been harvested by mid-December. When prompted, Henry simply replied, "I've got other plans."

* * *

Mother and Father,

I thank you once more for your concern, but I assure you, I am in high spirits. Do not worry yourselves over anything. I know for the last several months I have been mailing you letter after letter, package after package, about the crops, but I assure you that I am not obsessed. I spoke with the ones behind it and my eyes were suddenly opened to the cosmos.

You haven't written back in several weeks and neither have my sisters. I'm writing this to make sure my letters haven't been lost in the mail. I thwarted those men you sent to take me away and I would greatly appreciate it if you would not attempt such a thing again.

Sincerely,
Henry Jacobs

* * *

He ran through the field, tumbling over himself and knocking into the porch steps before clambering up and unlatching the screen door.

No time to write. Must record.

Bounding through the living room, he sprinted into the office and tore open the shelves of his desk, searching for a tape recorder. Success!

* * *

...and they are taking me tonight...there is no time to explain it all...you see...they aren't of this world...I know you'll think I'm mad, mom and pop, but this is the best way I can explain it to you...you see...their ship crashed here millennia ago on Pangaea...even aliens have ghosts and they have been haunting this Earth down through the various epochs of man's existence! I know this because they possessed me...they possessed me to bring together the final preparations...I didn't mean...I didn't want to kill those men you sent to help me!

Oh how I wish I could have spoken in my own voice and cried for help! I watched! I watched as it happened, but I was powerless...it was like watching it from a distance. I'm sorry...I'm so sorry...why me? Why my field? You see...I was right...I was right...the crop circles are a map! A map to the stars! They have been trapped here for millennia because the stars were not aligned properly...but now...only now can they leave, and they're taking me with them! They have been using me all along! I designed the circles! Under their control! I plotted out the designs! That's why no other footprints could be found! The lights were them!

The door! I hear the door opening! Oh,

they've come for me! Help me! Hideous...they're so hideous!

***

Printed in the Arcadia Gazette:
The search for former columnist, Henry Jacobs, has been called off after a fruitless six-month investigation...

About the author:

Jacob Henry Orloff has been writing horror fiction throughout several centuries in various past lives. In his current incarnation, he has been writing for nearly three years and is currently attending school to become an English major.

John Peters

For Want of a Ghost

It was a simple enough question.

"We're working on our Halloween edition and I wanted to do a piece on ghost stories around the lake. Do you know of any?"

"No."

Short, clipped, even hostile was the answer. Kurt Meyer had asked Aberdeen's chamber of commerce director, the clerk of the court (a self-styled local historian), both barbers in town, the head librarian, and the local newspaper editor.

Now he stood before the town mayor, a chance encounter on Main Street. Reportedly seventy-seven years old, Kurt looked at her with admiration for how well she had aged, or more appropriately, not aged. Short, perhaps five-two, Margaret Epperly was a slender woman. A few lines crossed her face, the beginnings of what would become wrinkles—what should be deep wrinkles, at her age—but Kurt thought she looked remarkable for a woman nearing the end of her eighth decade.

Doesn't look at day over fifty-five. Maybe younger.

Kurt had just posed the question to Mayor Epperly. They strolled together down Main Street's brick sidewalks, she on her way to the Aberdeen Courier's office to speak with the newspaper editor, he on his way to the Hardware Café, a tiny restaurant he believed to be the best kept secret in the Lake Lanier region.

She stopped walking. Her brows furrowed.

"Why would you ask such a question, young man?"

"October's coming up. You know, Halloween and such. We thought it would be—"

"We?"

"All of us at Lake Lanier Magazine. With Hallow—"

"Lake Lanier Magazine? Isn't that published in Little Rapids?"

"Yes ma'am, that's where our office is, but we cover the entire lake region. All five counties on the North Carolina and Virginia sides of the lake."

Mayor Epperly nodded.

"Anyway, we thought for our October edition one of our stories could be the ghosts of Lake Lanier. Only problem is, we can't find any."

Mayor Epperly chuckled.

"So you thought you'd come way out here for a haunting or two?"

"Well, it's not really way out here. Just a thirty-minute drive. Aberdeen is the oldest town in the region, so we do some coverage up here all year."

"Some coverage? Meaning when you can't find anything else to write about you slip this way?"

Kurt opened his mouth, but did not know what to say. There was not a lot of development in the entire region—small towns surrounded by rolling tobacco and cotton farms. If not for the lake, the area would be populated by nothing but sixth-generation families. He shrugged.

"What makes you think you'll have better luck here?"

"Aberdeen's older than the United States. Some of these beautiful homes predate the

Revolutionary War.   Like that house there," he
said, pointing across the courthouse square to a
home a block over from Main Street. The house was
but two stories, though so large Kurt imagined
the ceilings inside to be at least ten feet tall.
The Greek Revival structure was similar to many
homes dotting the lanes and avenues of Aberdeen,
with giant white columns standing guard around a
semi-circular front porch; black shutters lining
the floor length windows; expansive green lawn
shaded by magnolia trees and ancient oaks; all
surrounded by a knee-high stone wall.   Kurt had
never wanted to settle in a small town—settling
anywhere was not really in the plan—but the first
time he visited Aberdeen, *charming* was the word
that came to mind.

"That house is just screaming to be home to a
haunting. If not that one, then another. There's
got to be a ghost story or two floating around
town. Every time I ask someone about it, though,
it's as if I just told them I've been sleeping
with their sister."

Mayor Epperly chuckled again.   "Maybe that
ought to tell you something."

Kurt stared, not sure what she meant.

She leaned into him, rising on her toes.   A
bystander might think they were mother and son,
and that she was trying to plant one on his cheek.

"Come closer," she whispered. He stooped, and
then felt it—the soft wetness of her tongue,
slipping inside his ear.

Kurt jumped. He took three quick steps back,
body shuddering.

Mayor Epperly laughed, a loud, harsh cackle.

"What's wrong, deary?"

Kurt dug in his ear, as a seven year old might
trying desperately to wipe the cooties from his
first kiss.

"Come by my place later and we'll finish," she said, her voice a deep whisper.

"Mayor Epperly, I…" Words failed Kurt. He had absolutely nothing to say.

She laughed again. "Am I that repulsive?"

"Not, no, not repulsive," Kurt stuttered, his face flushing. "It's just…well…Mayor Epperly, you're old enough to be my grandmother."

"And?"

"There're just some things that just shouldn't happen."

"Yes, my dear, there are things that should never happen. Perhaps your ghost story is one of those."

She smiled, then walked away.

***

For the next week Kurt went about his duties—editing copy, interviewing peanut farmers for another October feature, working with his graphic artist on a cover design—but he could not get his mind off the mayor's warning.

He made more calls, checked Internet sites, but found no ghost stories in the region.

He talked with his publisher, Regina Coleman. Neither Regina nor Kurt were from the area, and each would probably be gone in two or three years. That was the transitory nature of the magazine world—you find a job, move in, make the publication look better, or at least different, for a couple of years, then move on.

"I don't get it," Kurt said, sitting in the uncomfortably hard chair in front of Regina's desk. "I've never, ever lived anywhere where there wasn't at least a half dozen ghost stories floating around."

"I'm sure they're there, Kurt," Regina said. She opened the bottom desk drawer, leaned back in her leather chair and propped her foot on the drawer. "You know these yokels, though. Odd lot, they are. Perhaps they like to keep this kind of thing hidden."

"Why? Most places think ghost stories bring tourists. There, it's almost like ghost is a four-letter word."

"Don't know what to tell you. But, we promo'd the story in our last issue, so you gotta come up with something."

"I know," Kurt sighed.

***

The next morning, with his deadline a week away, Kurt stood in the Aberdeen Funeral Home, one of three such parlors in the tiny town. *Never could understand that—town of only seven hundred yet three funeral homes.* Kurt forced himself to focus on Myron LaFoon, the chief undertaker.

"We don't really believe in ghosts in my line of work." Myron stood, walked around his desk. "I really have a lot to do, so if…"

"Five more minutes?"

Myron stopped. "Well, if you insist, you can follow me to the embalming room. We can continue chatting there."

Embalming room?

Myron stepped from his office and went off toward the rear of the building.

"Wait," Kurt called. He slipped into the hallway, watched Myron disappear through a darkened archway.

Oh geeze, hope I don't throw up. Legs unsteady, he pushed onward, following Myron. Kurt stepped through the alcove into a large circular room. The walls were lined with six doors—one shut just as Kurt stepped through the archway.

"Mr. LaFoon?"

Nothing.

Kurt eased over to the door. He reached for the handle, the metal cold against his fingers, and pulled the door open.

Then gasped.

In the center of the room was a stainless steel table. Hanging above was a round gleaming stainless steel light fixture. Next to the table was a tray with a dozen different instruments, most of which Kurt had no clue as to what their purpose might be. At this moment he really did not want to know.

On the table was a body. A woman. She wore a flower-print dress. She was barefoot.

"There you are," Myron said. "Come on in."

Kurt stepped through the doorway. The room started to spin. Kurt leaned against the wall, looked at Myron, focusing on his face, trying not to glance at the body.

"You okay?" Myron asked.

"Uh, yeah, fine. Can…can't you get in trouble for having me in here?"

"Not really," Myron said. He was leaning over the woman's remains, messaging her face. "Embalming is all done. Just have a few touches to finish."

Kurt watched as Myron picked up a tube. He squirted some white creamy substance on his hands, rubbed them together, then began working the cream into the woman's face. As he massaged, Myron moved from her left side to the end of the table, above her head, then around to her right.

"What are you doing?"

"Moisturizer. Have to keep the skin pliable until I'm done. I use a ton of this stuff. First thing I do, after washing the body, is apply moisturizer to the face, neck and hands. Then I have to do it again after filling her with embalming fluid, then a third time just before final preparations."

The room spun again. The edges of Kurt's vision turned gray.

"Uh…about the, um, ghosts," Kurt said, now staring slightly over Myron, trying to keep the body and Myron's work from his field of vision.

"Like I said, belief in ghosts aren't real big in my line of work."

"Yeah, but surely you've heard stories of—"

"Damn."

"What?" Kurt said, concerned.

"Her mouth won't open."

Kurt glanced down just in time to see Myron shift the woman's lower jaw to the right with one hand while pushing her head to the left with his other hand.

Snap.

The mouth opened.

★★★

"Mr. Meyer?"

Kurt opened his eyes. Peering down on him was Myron and another man, tall and gaunt, dressed in a black suit. *He looks like Lurch.* The theme from the Adams Family began running through Kurt's head. He pushed up on one elbow. A guttural sound, something between a gasp, a moan and a scream, escaped his throat when Kurt realized he was lying on a stainless steel table. He scrambled down, too fast, slapping his head against the light fixture. The blow knocked him off balance. Kurt reached out to steady himself and knocked the tray of instruments clanging to the floor.

"Jesus Christ," he muttered, pedaling backward, feet stepping furiously in a vain attempt to keep his balance. Kurt fell, butt first, on the concrete floor, bouncing once before coming to a rest. Myron and Lurch stood at the table, wide-eyed. The light fixture swung back and forth, alternating between bathing their faces in light, then shadow.

"You okay, Mr. Meyer?"

"Um, yeah." Kurt stood, pretending the past twenty seconds had never happened. "I…"

"Passed out," Myron said. "I couldn't rouse you, so my associate here, Benny Hester, helped me get you to one of our other tables."

Kurt looked around the room.

"In another room, Mr. Meyer. I didn't think it would be prudent for you to wake up next to a body."

Still too hazy to feel embarrassed, Kurt stepped toward the door. "My—"

Myron handed Kurt his notebook and pen.

Kurt smiled weakly.

"Perhaps we should finish this another time, Mr. Meyer?"

"Yeah, maybe so."

He stepped away, then whirled back to Myron. "Who was she?"

"Excuse me?"

"The woman. Who was she, how did she die?"

"Estelle Darcy, from Halifax. She was killed by her husband. He's in jail. Why do you ask?"

"Why is she having her funeral here, in Aberdeen, if she's from Halifax? That's thirty miles away."

Myron shrugged.

Kurt strode from the room, up the hallway, then glanced around to make sure no one could see him. He opened the door, the bell hanging above announcing his exit, then he shut the door while remaining inside the building.

Kurt looked at the viewing schedule posted in the foyer—Estelle Darcy was the only body in the home. He slipped into Myron's office, opened the file cabinet marked "2006-2009." Estelle Darcy's file was in there—Halifax resident, death by strangulation at the hands of her estranged husband. He looked at the next file, from a funeral two weeks earlier. Jacob Bollinger, residence listed as Little Rapids, cause of death attributed to a car accident. The next, from two months ago, was Tim Shelton, residence listed as New Brunswick—a town on the other side of the lake, *must be an hour's drive*—cause of death suicide.

He glanced through all dozen of the files for 2006 and 2007. *Not a single person from Aberdeen, and every one met a violent death.* He flipped through the final six months of 2005 and saw the records for eight funerals, none from Aberdeen, all meeting a brutal demise.

Kurt eased the drawer shut, then slipped through the front exit, careful to keep the bell over the door from ringing.

Inside the Aberdeen Funeral Home, Myron watched Kurt slip out. "He may be trouble. Benny, keep an eye on him."

***

Kurt stopped at the town's other two funeral homes, asking about ghost stories, using the visits to snoop around, learn what he could about their clientele. Neither of the undertakers knew of a single ghost story, and only one had a body, that of LeRoy Davis, shot down in a drunken dispute over a woman. The funeral director, Bryan Sommerville, told Kurt that LeRoy was from Little Rapids.

"He have family here in Aberdeen?"

"No, don't think he did," the director said. "Well, 'cept for his great-grandfather. I think he lives here."

"His great-grandfather? How old is he?"

"Don't rightly know."

"Why do so many people from out of town end up in Aberdeen for their funerals?" Kurt asked.

The man shrugged.

Kurt thanked him for his time, then left.

Bryan picked up the phone, punched in a number. "Myron? Bryan. That magazine editor you called about. He was here, asking questions."

***

A sudden, chilly wind sent dead leaves spiraling around Kurt. Dressed in short sleeves, he shuddered at the unexpected bite in the late summer air. He rubbed his arms, glanced at his watch—seven o'clock. Probably light enough to see well for another half hour.

Kurt started in what appeared to be the oldest section of the cemetery, where moss-covered gray sandstone markers jutted from the ground like ancient bones. Some were uneven, chunks of rock having crumbled out decades ago. A few carried remnants of dates and some wording, but most were blank, inscriptions blotted out by rain and snow and heat and time.

The earliest dates he could make out were for a couple of stones marking births in the 1780s, deaths shortly after the turn of the nineteenth century. Kurt worked his way across the cemetery— 1820s, 1840s, 1860s, by the time he reached the 1880s the stones where ghostly white, with well preserved etchings. He continued looking, hoping to find some clue as to where those buried had lived. Writing down inscription after inscription, Kurt knew he could at least take this information to the courthouse, learn where these people had lived, perhaps how they died.

Wait a minute.

He flipped through his notes.

Smith. Marshall. Pearson. Gallan. Martin. Haislip. Pendergrass.

Not a single duplicate name. No husband-wife burials, no parent-child burials, no—"

Kurt noticed movement to his left. He turned, caught a glimpse of a figure swinging something. Pain exploded in his head. His vision went black. Vaguely, as if waking from a dream, Kurt felt a sharp ache spread over his head, down his neck, then he sensed his body falling, felt it thud to the ground.

***

Light.

Blinding light.

That was the first sensation to register in Kurt's consciousness. The second was an agonizing, sickening headache. He squinted against the light, raised his hand, then...*Where's my hand?* Panic rising, Kurt tried to sit. Nothing happened. He could not even move his head.

A shadow blotted the light. Kurt's eyes took a few seconds to adjust. It was Myron. And

Benny Hester. And the directors from the town's other two funeral homes, all standing over him.

"Don't worry, Mr. Meyer, this won't take too long."

Kurt tried to speak. Nothing happened. All he could do was move his eyes side to side.

"This is a bit of a treat, Mr. Meyer. And it will go so much better for you, too. I suspect we'll be seeing your spirit show up in town soon and this will be somewhat of an orientation for you. Hopefully, you'll remember all we say here, skip over that difficult adjustment period so many have when they come to Aberdeen."

Myron talked as he worked. Kurt saw tubes, a needle. Myron reached up, grabbed a metal hose hanging from a fixture in the ceiling and pressed a button. Ice cold water splashed across Kurt's body. He realized he was naked.

Myron finished spraying him, pulled the tray over. Kurt heard the clang of metal instruments.

What are you doing? Kurt cried, but the words echoed only in his head, no sound escaping his lips.

"As you deduced, Mr. Meyer, Aberdeen is a ghost town in the truest sense of the word," Myron said. He pulled a tube with a long intravenous needle at the end from a rack hanging over the table. Myron leaned over, out of Kurt's line of vision. He spoke slowly, as if concentrating on something other than his words. "There are no ghosts stories to be told, anywhere in lake country."

Kurt felt a pinprick in his chest, then fire erupted in his veins, raced through his body. Vision blurred as tears welled in his eyes.

"Oh, yes, I suspect this does hurt quite a lot. I do wish you could speak. I'd love to hear you describe the sensations. I'd—gentlemen, look at this." Myron waved the others over. They stood, staring at Kurt. "Look at how the skin is turning red, in streaks, following the embalming fluid."

No, Kurt tried to scream. His eyes burned. He felt hot. His heart pounded, faster and faster, each beat sending shards of agony across his chest. Kurt's vision of the room danced unevenly as his eyes flicked back and forth.

"Oh, forgive me, Mr. Meyer, let me explain. We are embalming you. Alive. Harsh, yes, but I tell you there's not an undertaker in North America who hasn't dreamt of this at least once, wondered what it would be like. You've given us a singularly unique opportunity.

"Now, back to your questions about ghosts stories. Nearly everyone in Aberdeen is a ghost." Myron picked up a long metal tool, pointed and sharp at one end, joined to a rubber hose at the other. He again bent from Kurt's line of sight. Shortly, Kurt felt a stabbing pain in his stomach. Something inside, digging around, tearing. Myron returned, still working the instrument in Kurt's stomach.

"This is a trocar, Mr. Meyer. What I'm doing now is puncturing your organs."

Kurt felt something let loose, as if his bowels had emptied themselves, only the sensation ran through his torso, right up to his neck. "We drain the organs, then pump them full of formaldehyde. Generally we wait until the embalming is complete, but the chance to see it work on a live person..." Myron did not finish his sentence, as if too awed by the thought.

"Anyway, the ghost story thing is quite simple."

A wave of nausea rolled through Kurt's body.

"A long, long time ago, even before America was a country, people around these parts decided they didn't like ghosts and whatnot spooking around at night."

Kurt coughed. The reflex started down in his chest and moved upward, expelling air from his mouth, unlike any cough he had ever felt, jolts of pure torture reverberating through his body.

"Seems they had a bad experience with a local man. The story goes he was unjustly imprisoned, then killed. The man's spirit returned, and as you can imagine, caused great havoc on those responsible for his death."

Another wave of nausea washed over Kurt. The taste of bile rose in his throat. The burning had spread throughout his body, the tearing sensation in his torso excruciating every time Myron moved the trocar.

"A few of the village elders got together, consulted with a couple of their slaves from the Caribbean, some with knowledge of voodoo and the black arts, and banished the ghost—all ghosts—to a small plot of land next to the Aberdeen cemetery."

Kurt felt vomit coming, forcing its way up his throat. He tried reaching to his mouth, sitting up, rolling, but his body was dead, only his mind still clung to life.

"Didn't take long 'fore all the villages around this area learned what had happened, asked the slaves to do the same thing for them."

Vomit filled Kurt's mouth, forced itself through his lips. Involuntary he gasped, pulling some of the substance into his throat, into his esophagus.

"So from then on, every time a person met a violent end, one of those deaths likely to cause problems with a restless spirit, the body is shipped here, buried in Aberdeen, spirit trapped within the town's limits."

Kurt's vision turned gray. He struggled to breathe, to cough, to clear his throat. His thoughts, panic-filled just seconds ago, slowed. *I'm. Dying.*

"Pretty soon, the town was so full of dead folks, the live ones moved on out. Just us funeral directors left now, among all the…Mr. Meyer? Mr. Meyer?" Myron sighed. "Sorry fellows, think he's gone. Damn, we hadn't even gotten to the orifice stuffing…"

The words ceased.

***

Kurt woke, lying on a fresh mound of dirt. He rolled off and saw it was a freshly filled grave, his name etched on the bone-white stone protruding from the ground. In the distance, silhouetted against the setting sun were the outlines of Aberdeen's Main Street buildings.

Kurt walked toward them, and suddenly felt as if Aberdeen would always be his home.

About the author:
John Peters' fiction has been published in the Stoker-nominated Horror Library Vol. 3, Dark Recesses, Down in the Cellar, and elsewhere. He recently was named nonfiction editor at Dark Recesses, and works fulltime as a newspaper editor. John lives in the mountains of Southwest Virginia with his wife and their five children. Visit him at johnpeters2.webs.com/.

Jessica A. Weiss

Emily's Lake

Like you, the anchor is lost forever, somewhere in the lake. The boat bottom grates across the rocky shore, sending shivers through my body. Like when my third grade teacher would scratch her nails across the chalkboard to get my attention. She was a stupid woman, too. Nothing I can do about it now.

The caress of the late afternoon breeze is pleasant. It's rustling the leaves, my hair, rippling the lake's surface, and it feels wonderful on my flushed cheeks. I didn't realize how much work this was going to be. I'm really worn out.

The air is cool, comforting and welcome.

Now that I have the boat securely on shore, and sure it won't drift, I can look around and really enjoy my accomplishments. Everything here is alive, full of spring, and radiating hope. So beautiful and peaceful. Yes, very peaceful. I want to etch this place, this moment, in my memory. Something to hang on to later.

To think, this has always been your favorite place. Fitting, since it is so much like you. As if you were this place stitched into flesh and blood. Just the thought of you entwined forever with this lake makes me smile. I know this pleasant feeling can't last, but right now I am pleased.

Emily, this is your lake, your retreat. Can you see how much you are like this moment? Of course not. The simple beauty of nature seems to elude you. You never could appreciate what you had, and now you never will.

My tragic beauty, let me explain.

You hair, so much like the soft tones of the trees swaying along the shore line, with many shades of brown, and tinted by the wind, rain and sunlight. Softness of falled leaves that float on the water's surface, before rotting and turning to slime. How I loved the feel of your hair, the one time I wrapped my fingers in it.

Sunset has started, the sun's rays highlighting the lapping waves. Oh, so bright and wonderful—like your smile. It lit up the darkest days, as sunlight bursts through storm clouds. To see you smile was heaven to me, Emily. Did you know that? No, you didn't.

You never smiled at me.

Have you ever seen a lake this shade of dark blue, only slightly green around the edges? Solid, yet soft. Exactly like your eyes—eyes that looked at everything and saw nothing. How you captivated everyone with your look.

Oh, Emily, do you see?

That's right. You can't.

Did you feel that? A trout jumped, rippling the surface and sending out vibrations when it landed. My heart always jumped for you, Emily. You send frigid currents through my veins. I can still feel them.

I watched you when you were here, on this very rock—dreaming, listening, loving. Always loving. Always someone new.

I hated them.

How could you let them do that to you? They never really loved you—not the way that I do.

Have I proved that to you today? Do you doubt that I would do anything for you?

Look, Emily. There's an egret swooping low over the water's surface. He's calling for his lost mate. Sounds so lonely—just like me. All those nights calling out for you, needing you. But you had flown away. You never answered my call.

Cold, very cold. My hands don't like it, but I have to. I must. When your hands are dirty, you have to clean them.

You made me dirty, Emily. Touching you made my hands very dirty—but your lake will clean them again.

Do you see how the water turns red? So pretty as it swirls in the blue ripples. The sun has set the water on fire.

Fire.

No, fire isn't right for me. Wasn't good enough for you, either, Emily.

This is a fitting place for you, my dear. A fit and proper place. You spent so much time here on the sun and moon lit shore. It's only right that you spend eternity here.

I will always remember this place, this day, you.

I can hear them coming, can you?

No, you can't.

They must've been to your house. They have seen the mess we left behind in our haste to leave.

They know.

But they are too late—for you.

I will go with them quietly.

There is no reason to fight them. They won't understand, even if I were to try and explain. They won't believe me.

It's okay—neither did you.

But you are safe from the world, where no one can hurt you. No more pain for Emily, only peace.

And you can't ignore me anymore, Emily.

About the author:

Jessica A Weiss lives on the Southeastern Seaboard with her husband, children and various animals. When she isn't busy with them, she writes as much as she can. You can find her writing blog at The Writers Side Of The Looking Glass (thewriterssideofthelookingglass.blogspot. com/).

K.M. Rees

Control

Elisabeth needed time to reflect on her life, and found herself driving a long, lonely highway to gain perspective. She had spent the last thirty years in a fog, allowing everyone to control every aspect of her life—her family, friends, boyfriends, employers—but it was going to stop. Her best friend's recent betrayal still stung, and it sank in that she was in charge of her own destiny.

The thought brought an all-too-new smile to her lips as she realized she had finally gained control.

The late afternoon sun was still visible as she closed in on Woolf, a small, desolate town that always ignited a tingle of curiosity to burn across her skin—it could have been the solitude of the town, for it was at least an hour from any services, or perhaps it was the difficulty she had in understanding why thirteen people would chose to reside in such barren conditions.

Most of the houses in Woolf were abandoned years ago, leaving behind precarious formations of decaying wood and weathered glass. The few existing habitants resided in single-wide trailers in various stages of decomposition, courtesy of the blistering winds and smoldering summer rays readily found in the western Panhandle of Nebraska.

Broken and beaten cars littered the grassland, some newer than others, leaving the impression that Woolf was actually more of a car graveyard than a town. The only obvious geological structure in the area consisted of large rock outcroppings, suggestively laid out like the jagged spine of a colossal demon embarking on its journey home.

Elisabeth pulled her car over to the side of the road—even though she was sure she could have stopped dead center and not disturbed another traveler. She fished through her glove box and pulled out a small digital camera to capture the morose scenery for posterity.

A few yards from her car, she focused on the paramount rock formation. After snapping a few photos, she placed her hand over the top of the camera to increase the visibility of the preview pictures recorded on her digital equipment. She groaned when she saw each picture was flawed with a wispy smudge around the formation.

With a heavy sigh, Elisabeth returned to the driver's seat to continue her journey. She reached up to turn over the car's engine, but the keys were no longer in the ignition.

That's odd.

She stared at the empty ignition, and then felt along the floor.

Nothing.

She opened the door and stood to pat herself down.

Nothing.

She traced the few steps she had taken for the photographs, but could not locate the keys. Hands on her hips, she scanned the area. *Where in the world could they be?*

A flash of light caught Elisabeth's eye as she looked past her vehicle toward Woolf. About a hundred yards from her stood a young girl, dressed in tattered clothes, with her arm held high, and a set of familiar keys dangling from her crusty fingers. Licking her lips, the girl used her free hand to beckon Elisabeth forward.

"We wanna play with you," sang the girl through a malevolent smile. Without thought, Elisabeth walked toward the girl, intent on retrieving her car keys. The girl giggled and slipped behind the door of an abandoned, ramshackle shack.

"Please come out here! I'm running behind schedule and I do not have time to play," Elisabeth lied.

"Heeheehee."

"Listen, I promise I will stop on my way back through if you come out here right now and give me the keys. I'll even bring you something. A doll or candy or pop. How does that sound?"

Silence.

Elisabeth opened the door and scanned the one room shack. The girl was gone. *Slipped through the back window, or maybe hiding behind the door.* She stepped inside to peer around the room. The door slammed shut behind her, and a large man, bearing the same malevolence-infused grin as the little girl, said, "But we want to play now."

His eyes were alive and feral, and he grabbed Elisabeth by the wrist as she turned to run, thrusting her body against the wall, using his considerable weight to restrict her limbs.

Elisabeth realized that in one moment, she had lost the one thing she had gained to guide her fate—control.

Tears streaked down her cheeks as she begged for freedom. Her pleas were answered by a fat tongue slurping up her face, licking off the moisture. "Mmmmm. You're gonna taste good when we are done with you." The man grabbed a fistful of her hair and dragged her out the door.

He yanked her past the trailers, through the tall grass, and around to the opposing side of the same rock outcropping she had used as the center of her marred photographs. Eleven people of various ages had gathered—including the little girl, who placed an easily recognizable object on top of an eclectic pile of assorted keys.

Her meaty captor pinned Elisabeth against the rock wall. She almost fainted when she spied the steel chains bolted to the boulder's surface. Within minutes, each wrist was clamped and she was shackled, impotent, and terrified.

Hope lit up her chest for a brief moment when she saw a man off in the distance. She choked out a desperate call for help, but was cut off when she realized the man was in the process of pushing her car in with the rest of the abandoned vehicles.

A young man stood in front of her, gaining the attention of her captor. "You always get to catch them. I never get to chase and have any fun."

"You can have the next one. We'll be needing another one soon 'cuz this one's kinda scrawny and probably'l only last us a week."

"You've said that before," the teenager whined. "Just unhook this one and let me chase her around a bit. Where's she gonna go? She can't hide out here. Then when I catch her we can start taking her apart."

Elisabeth's eyes opened just enough to think about what she heard—*unhook, chase, take…apart.* Vomit thrust its way through her mouth and onto the rust-splattered ground.

The large man growled under his breath, but unhooked the chains. "Hurry up and have your fun. We want our fun, too."

For a moment, Elisabeth did not know what to do. The young man had been right—there was no place she could go, no place she could hide. But she felt something swell inside her, something delicate, and she realized that she had regained a small amount of control. It may have only been a sliver of power, but it was enough to seal her fate.

"Run, girl, run," teased the teenage boy.

Through a cacophony of jeering, Elisabeth clamored up the jagged rock formation until she reached its zenith, and from that ledge she jumped, joining the demon on its journey home.

About the author:

Originally from Colorado, K.M. Rees currently teaches high school English, Speech, and Drama in a rural Nebraska community. "Control" is her first publication.

Adrian Ludens

Beneath Kent's Bed

Everybody knows someone who's crazy.

Let me rephrase that—lots of people know someone who may be a little eccentric, but not many people actually know anyone who is truly insane. I'm talking totally unhinged.

The guy I'm thinking of was a little eccentric before the incident. Now, thanks to me, Kent Norman has been declared a danger to himself and others, and is currently heavily sedated as a resident of Custer Sanitarium.

My name's Monty Durfee, by the way.

I know what you're asking—what the hell did I do to send this guy off the deep end. It was an accident, I promise you that much.

I didn't do *any* of it deliberately.

And what happened was pretty damned hard on me, too.

It was hot as hell the day it happened. I'd driven my old Dodge east out of Sturgis on South Dakota Highway 34, the windows rolled down, the pedal to the floor. It had to be about ninety-five degrees, and I figured my speed could match the temperature. I had plans to meet some friends in Rapid City for steaks and brews.

About four miles north of Kent's place on Little Alkali Road, the Dodge's radiator overheated. I don't own a cell phone, and even if I did, the reception out there is pretty iffy.

The merciless sun beat down, browning the grass to a crisp. It didn't take long for my arms to redden and for my bald spot to burn.

I wish I'd brought a hat.

I spent about an hour shuffling down the gravel road that led me to Kent's farm. Not one single vehicle passed. I wasn't surprised. Kent's people hadn't exactly settled on prime land.

Finally, I crossed the road and hoisted a leg over the rusted strand of barbed wire that marked the Norman Farm property line. I cut through the line of scraggly jack pines on the west end of the farm—we call it a shelter belt because it's supposed to serve as a windbreak during the winter—and shambled toward the old house through a fallow field filled with the rusted skeletons of every car, truck and tractor the man had ever owned. You could practically trace the evolution of the American automobile right there in the field.

I crunched over the gravel path that served as a driveway, past a broken refrigerator standing sentry in the yard, and mounted the steps to Kent's front door. I wiped sweat off my face, and then rapped on the door.

No one responded.

I pressed my forehead against the nearest rectangular window beside the door and peered inside. The only movement came from a few horseflies circling the air above the cluttered kitchen table. I kicked an empty beer can across the yard and looked in the ramshackle wooden shed where I figured Kent parked his truck.

It was empty.

Would he mind if I went inside and helped myself to some water? Hard to say. Kent's place wasn't my original destination—Rapid City was.

We weren't exactly friends, either. We never associated much at all. Kent might get a little pissed that I barged in without permission, but he would get over. And I didn't care if he didn't. Like I said, we weren't close. Besides, who'd be asshole enough to begrudge a thirsty man a drink of water?

I tried the knob. The door was unlocked. I shoved it open, ducked inside, and made a beeline for the kitchen sink. The inside of Kent's house wasn't as cool as I'd hoped, but the water was ice cold and fine as wine as far as I was concerned. I polished off two and a half glasses before I even thought to glance around.

Kent's a lifelong bachelor who'd taken to keeping to himself as much as he could, and not an overly friendly guy. He stands about six-foot-three and weighs about two forty. It's all muscle. He has a big, bushy gray beard, gaunt features, and what I called "coke-bottle glasses" when I was a kid.

Not long ago, Kent was a hell-raising biker. Coming home one night on his supped-up orange motorcycle, and not wearing a helmet, he wiped out on a patch of loose gravel and went sliding along on his face before cart-wheeling into the ditch. He spent a few weeks in the Meade County Hospital. Should've been more, but the doctors couldn't convince him to stay. Most everyone in town thought he'd end up looking like The Phantom of the Opera or that comic book super-villain with the scarred up face.

We were all wrong. His face healed up rather nicely, and except for anosmia, which I found out is a fancy word for losing your sense of smell, Kent bears no physical scars from the accident.

Emotional scars tell another story.

Kent stopped riding his bike, and traded the motorcycle for the pickup truck. He even buckles up. And the booze went away for a while.

From what I saw, Kent's life started to revolve around exercising and going to church activities every Sunday morning, and Wednesday and Saturday nights. That's where he first met Gina Dowling. She became his "lady friend" and that lasted for over two years.

One time while I stood in line at the post office, I overheard two old bags gossiping that Kent had brought up the subject of marriage with Gina. She'd been reluctant for reasons only she knew, and had told him no. Kent took the rejection mighty hard.

Pretty soon after that, Gina Dowling left town completely. Nobody saw her around. The general consensus was that she took the bus back home to her family, though no one was sure where she was originally from. No one had seen or heard from her since—and that was over a year ago.

How did Kent take her leaving? Nobody knew. He's not the type to share his feelings with anyone. He never even admitted that he asked her to marry him. Maybe he didn't care, but I never brought it up in a conversation. Kent still had enough of that ugly old temper to make folks not want to pry on a touchy subject.

Kent stopped attending church, as that was the place he most associated with Gina. Then he started drinking and brawling again.

That all happened a year ago. And that brings us back—or maybe forward—to me, standing in the middle of Kent Norman's kitchen.

Want to hear something crazy? I'd known him for over fifteen years, but I hadn't ever been inside Kent's house. Not once. I got this giddy urge to start snooping around, and it was too hard to fight.

A little cluster of breakfast dishes sat in the drying rack. A selection of magazines lay strewn across the kitchen table. Farming was the main topic of interest.

I moved on.

The floor boards squealed their protest as I walked, like they resented my presence. I peeked in the cupboards and found cups, dishes, old Tupperware. A bottle of whiskey was tucked into the corner of the cabinet above the refrigerator.

I resisted the urge to pour myself a shot or three.

Kent owned a television, but it was covered with an old navy blue blanket. A tattered recliner hunched in one corner. Next to it stood a small end table, pockmarked with cigarette burns. Behind that, a yellow lamp towered over the other furniture.

The air was stale, a little gamey. I turned to face the nearest wall where several pictures hung. I was surprised to see Gina Dowling in most of them, even after everything that had happened. I stepped closer, noticing two things— although everything else in Kent's house had the grimy look and feel of a lifetime of accumulated dust, the pictures of Gina were wiped clean, and Gina wore the same frumpy green floral print dress in all the pictures.

Did that woman own any other clothes? I snickered at her expense.

Following the narrow hallway brought me to the bathroom, which I only glanced in, then to Kent's bedroom. I could see countless dust mites floating in the beans of sunlight like inmates milling around a prison yard.

A chest of drawers occupied one corner of the room, and opposite the foot of the bed was double-doors half-open, exposing a mishmash of flannel work shirts, denim coveralls, winter parkas and the like. Fly strips hung in all four corners, and were matted with black dots.

Disgusted, I glanced at the bed and was seized by the hilarious notion that Kent had squirreled away a nudie magazine or two under his mattress. Next thing I knew, I'd stooped, intending to lift the mattress to sneak a peek. Then I heard the front door squeal open.

Guilt at being caught gripped me. I was too far away to reach the bathroom, which would have been a plausible excuse for being inside Kent's home uninvited. I sure couldn't casually say, "How ya doin', Kent! Just takin' the grand tour."

I did what any normal person would do—I dropped to the floor and squirmed under the bed.

Kent plodded down the hall and straight into the bathroom. For a second, I thought I could make a break for it, but the stream of piss sounded so loud that I realized he hadn't closed the door.

Hell, living alone, he had no reason to.

I waited.

Kent ambled back up the hall to the kitchen and I heard him fill a glass with water from the tap. Then he did the last think I wanted him to do—he came back into the bedroom and flopped on to the bed.

I had a moment of claustrophobic panic as the box spring sagged toward me. Box springs shouldn't sag at all, but this one looked old enough for Lincoln to have slept on, and it was pretty well shot.

The trapped feeling gave way to another kind of fear as I felt a strong itching sensation welling up from deep in my sinuses.   I pinched my nose, pushing upward with my index finger and thumb, a trick I'd learned in school to avoid sneezing that I still used sometimes at the movies.   The urge to sneeze disappeared and I vowed to breathe through my mouth as long as I remained hidden.

Kent tossed and turned, then began to sob.   I felt a greasy sense of shame.   I had violated Kent's privacy by snooping around his home, but I felt even weirder about listening to his grief.

He continued to cry, pounding the mattress with his fists.   The situation was quickly becoming unbearable, wedged under his bed.   I ground my teeth and clenched my own fists in frustration.   I turned my head toward the far wall and my heart stopped.

Less than three feet away lay a human corpse.

I jerked a hand to my face again, but this time, I chomped down on my hand to keep from screaming.   I noticed no pain in my hand, though. I was too focused on the hideous grin and sunken black eye sockets of what once had been a face staring accusingly up at the box springs.   I was utterly revolted, and my head swam.

Then my mind took a little vacation, and I passed out.

When I came to, my muscles were screaming in protest.   My right arm felt numb from my bicep down because of how it was angled against my body.   When I tried to take my hand out of my mouth, I couldn't move it at first.   I opened my mouth wider and my palm limply fell free.   In the waning light of the late afternoon, I could see that it was encrusted with dried blood.

I'd really clamped down hard. I wondered how my teeth looked. Probably like a fucking vampire.

Cutting off the circulation had obviously helped staunch any additional blood flow, and had numbed the pain. Now that I had moved it, though, my hand began throbbing and the length of my arm felt like it was grilling on a spit.

This'll sound crazy—but to take my mind off my discomfort, I looked at the skeleton. The remains appeared to be in the dry decay state of decomposition. I saw only bone, wispy hair and the tattered remnants of a dress.

Something about the dress tickled my brain. It was a floral print that could have been green at one tim...

Oh, sweet Jesus!

It was Gina Dowling. There wasn't a doubt in my mind. Kent hunted her down, or maybe she was dumb enough to come knocking on his door. I didn't know. All I knew for sure was that Kent was one crazy and sadistic bastard for stuffing her body under his bed for a souvenir.

I was trembling. I had broken out in a cold sweat fueled by revulsion and fear. The skeleton had taken a back seat to my new terror—discovery and subsequent murder at the hands of a madman.

Nausea swept over me and I closed my eyes. My hand throbbed angrily. I wanted to gag, thanks to the coppery taste of blood lingering in my mouth, and I longed for water. Some of my muscles ached while others burned. I wondered if I'd even be able to move fast enough to escape if the opportunity arose.

Above me, I could hear Kent muttering in uneasy sleep. I knew his present location—that was

something to be thankful for. I tried to wriggle
my way out from under the bed, but the floor below
me creaked in protest and Kent snorted.

I froze, acrid sweat burning my eyes, until
his breathing became regular again. I didn't
like how easily he'd woken, so I resolved to stay
where I was for the time being.

I looked again at my lifeless companion. Fate
had brought us together, and it was apparent that
the situation would keep us that way for a while.

I made it a game to pass the time without
losing my mind.

What did he do to you, Gina? How did you die?

I contemplated several grisly endings for
Kent's former girlfriend. Then fate stepped
in with answers. I heard the bed springs creek
loudly as Kent rolled closer to the wall. To my
astonishment, the wooden crossbeams, nailed to the
frame for support, sagged downward significantly.
Under the right side of the bed, the beam pressed
against my chest slightly, but under the left
side, the board was firmly pressed against Gina's
crushed skull.

I raised my right arm, stretched it taut, and
felt down the back of the skull with my fingers.
Small tufts of brittle hair still clung there,
but it disintegrated as I touched it. My middle
finger pressed against a jagged crack and followed
it downward. I dislodged a bone fragment and
felt it move away from my fingers and into the
hollowed confines of the skull.

I felt like I was palming the most macabre
piece of pottery in the world.

Gina had been stowed away for a year or so,
since she had disappeared. Why would Kent hide
her remains under her bed and let her rot right
beneath him?

She had decomposed where she lay—the discoloration of the carpet and the abundance of dead bugs on the fly strips were evidence enough of that.

The realization hit me. The anosmia—Kent had no sense of smell. That was how he could stand it.

Hang up some fly strips and rest easy, you crazy bastard! You've got anosmia, so what do you care?

Uh-knows-mia...a-noose-me-yah...an-owes-me-a...

I played with the word until I fell into a shallow doze.

I dreamed of sitting at a large table, with serving dishes being passed from person to person. Gina Dowling sat across from me. As I watched, her skin shriveled and disappeared. Her eyes fell and dangled from their sockets, her lips dried and receded.

Kent was sitting beside me, but not in a regular chair—he was strapped into an electric chair. He stared forlornly at his plate. On his head perched the copper electrode helmet.

"You need to get him out of that chair," a woman's voice said, tired and heartbroken. I jerked my head and was astonished to see Gina's skeletal jaw opening and closing in time with the words. The teeth clicked and clattered, but in my mind I heard her final plea. "You know he doesn't really belong there."

I jolted awake, smacking my forehead on the box spring frame and inhaling a cloud of dust mites. A violent coughing fit swept over me. If Kent was still in the room, I was a dead man.

I tensed and listened. I heard water running. He was taking a shower.

I threw a wary glance at the skull and the crossbeam.

Oh, my God, I know what happened.

Before I could move, Kent padded back into his bedroom and sat down on the edge of the bed. From my vantage point, I watched him pull on faded jeans and a pair of gray athletic socks. I kept still and heard him remove a shirt from a hanger in the closet.

I wasn't afraid of Kent anymore.

He sighed as he left the bedroom. He paused to click off the bathroom light, then shuffled to the living room. Finally, I heard the front door open and close.

I waited for the muffled thump of the driver-side door to his pickup slamming shut, then the engine roaring to life.

My muscles screamed as I wriggled free from my confinement. I shakily stood, tried to take a few steps, and flopped face first onto the bed. I gave myself a few minutes to build up some stamina and to get the blood flowing again.

When I tried standing again, my legs held, and after a couple tentative steps, I was in the bathroom, fumbling with my pants. My bladder felt like it was going to burst. I pissed for so long that I started to get paranoid about him coming back and catching me midstream. After what seemed like forever, I finished, flushed and crept back into the hallway.

By the time I reached the living room, I felt faint. I stumbled into Kent's worn recliner, closed my eyes, and waited for the fog to lift.

I jumped at a sudden sound, and then sprung out of the recliner when someone approached the entrance to the house. The door flew open and I stood, gaping foolishly, and coming up blank.

"Monte Durfee?" He squinted at me, his breath reeking of whiskey. "What the hell are you doin' in my house?"

I couldn't think of a damned thing to say.

Kent leaned toward me, scowling. The smell of single malt singed my nose hairs.

"You tryin' to steal from me?"

I shook my head in denial, but he shot one big paw out and grabbed my shirt, slamming his other fist into my face. A nauseating crunch exploded in my ears as the cartilage in my nose collapsed. Hot blood sprayed in every direction.

"Nobody steals from me, you little weasel!"

My eyes streamed tears. Kent swung again, and something like fireworks exploded inside my eyes. I raised my arms in a feeble attempt at covering my face, but it was useless. My knees buckled and I would have fallen if Kent had let go of my shirt.

"Any last words, thief?" Kent growled.

"Kent, stop!" I was sure that in his rage he would keep pounding on me until I was dead. I thought of the corpse under his bed and said the only thing I could think of to get him off of me. "Gina's…in there…under the bed…"

I pointed feebly.

Kent froze, one fist still wrapped in my shirt, the other cocked in midair. His mouth hung open in disbelief, but his eyes widened and seemed to bore right through my brain.

He must have decided I was telling the truth, although he couldn't understand what I really meant. He relaxed his grip, and I dropped like a rag doll onto the dusty carpet. Kent's pounding footsteps receded and everything in my world faded to black.

* * *

Sheriff Ryan Salazar was waiting in my hospital room when I woke up. He had a lot of questions

and a few answers. I helped him out as best
I could, filling him in about my experience in
Kent's house.

Later, after I got released from the hospital,
and had healed up some, I downed a few cold ones
with Deputy Eddie Johnson at Gunsey's Bar. We
decided that after the marriage proposal, Gina
snuck into Kent's house. Maybe she changed her
mind or came to apologize.

Kent wasn't home, and she set about snooping,
and eventually found herself in a position very
similar to mine—overwhelming panic at being
caught somewhere she wasn't supposed to be. She
did what I did—hid under the bed, right under the
part of the box spring that sagged the most.

Kent barreled into his room—all two hundred
and forty pounds of him—and flopped down on the
weak part of the bed and crushed her skull. Gina
must have died instantly, never making a sound.
And Kent never even knew it.

When he found his missing girlfriend, Kent went
ape-shit. He tore the place apart. Literally.
Eddie says that I'm damn lucky to be alive. He
thinks Kent must have forgot me lying there on
the floor.

Sheriff Salazar is the one who took Kent
down by putting two slugs from his old Colt .45
"slabside" into one of Kent's knees. Even then
Kent kept coming. Eddie said when he got the
radio call for backup, Salazar told him to bring
a tranquilizer gun—the one they used on wild
animals.

So, that's the series of events that led Kent
Norman to be deemed a threat to himself and
others, and why he now spends his time sedated at
Custer Sanitarium. And now you know why it's my
fault. I like to think that by explaining what

I'd seen under Kent's bed that I saved him from the electric chair.

I don't pat myself on the shoulder too much, though.

These days I'm prone to crying fits and I can never seem to drink enough. I have a lot of trouble sleeping in my bed now, too. I have to fight off the urge to check under it every few minutes. I usually drift off in my recliner.

Sometimes I dream.

In my dreams, my friends are gathered around the dinner table. This time the seat across from me – the one Gina had occupied – is empty.

Maybe that means she is at rest.

Kent is still beside me, but instead of being in an electric chair, he's bound up in a straightjacket. He thrashes in his chair, groaning and gibbering while the rest of us eat, but at least he's alive and at the table.

That's something to be thankful for.

Isn't it?

About the author:
Adrian Ludens is a radio personality in the Black Hills of South Dakota. His short fiction has appeared in Alfred Hitchcock Mystery Magazine, Morpheus Tales, ThugLit, Trail of Indiscretion, and many others. Visit him at www.myspace.com/adrianludens.

D. Nathan Hilliard

Storm Chase

Bernie March leaned on the old sawhorse by the tool shed, and stared through the gathering gloom at the white figure down the hill. It flapped crazily in the surging wind, yet still stood fixed in one spot near the back corner of the plowed field. The roar of the gale swept away any noise that might have come from it. Hurricane Carla loomed from the south, the heavy clouds already turning the late afternoon into near night, and he needed to get down there to where he parked his old tractor. If the Brazos River rose in the hurricane, it could wash the tractor away, and he couldn't afford to replace it.

The problem was, the white figure near the tractor stood exactly where he buried Charlotte, three years ago.

Bernie chewed a knuckle and squinted against the blast. The wind already smelled heavy of moisture. Soon the rain would come, and it would be too late. The radio inside blared about the approaching monster storm, and warned everybody to seek shelter. He needed to get that tractor quickly…but he felt no desire to confront the figure he could feel staring back up the hill at him from her anonymous grave in the rows below. At this distance, the logical part of his mind told him it could be a lot of things…but his gut knew better. He had buried Charlotte in her wedding dress and wrapped her body in a white bed sheet…just like the one flapping from the pale figure rocking back and forth at the other end of the field.

Indecision tore at him, his practical nature at war with the primal fear of the unknown. A spatter of wind whipped drops stung his face. Time was running out, and if he intended to insure he still owned a tractor after tomorrow, then he needed to act immediately. No tractor meant no spring planting, and he would lose everything. He must go down there.

Down there where the figure waited.

Blam!

Bernie almost jumped out of his skin at the sound, and wheeled to see Molly coming down the back steps of the little farm house. She held her slender wrist and flexed her fingers where the wind tore the back screen door from her grasp. Her delicate features bore a vexed grimace, as if the cyclone raging around them existed only to irritate her. She looked as out of place on this lonely farm as a china figurine in a ragdoll collection. Bernie wondered why she even bothered to come outside.

"Bernie!" she yelled through the blast, "the power just went out!" She gripped the useless scarf she wore on her head, while at the same time trying to shield her face from the flying dirt and twigs. "What are you still doing out here?"

Words could not express how little Bernie cared about the power at the moment. He settled for pointing down the hill instead. The distant object remained in place, cloth flapping wildly in the roaring murk.

"Huh?" she frowned and came over to him. Looking in the gestured direction, she squinted against the storm's onslaught, "oh, I see it. What is that?"

He did not say anything, preferring her to arrive at her own answer. She helped him bury Charlotte, so she had the same facts at her disposal that he did. Maybe she would come up with something he did not think of. Perhaps her quick mind could produce a simple explanation that would free him to retrieve his tractor without fear.

Instead, she suddenly gripped his arm, her nails biting into chilled skin.

"Oh God, Bernie! What *is* that?"

The hint of hysteria in her voice told him she already had her answer, and it looked a whole lot like his. He glanced up to see her already pale face now almost white with fear. Her wide eyes met his, begging him to answer her with anything but her own conclusion.

"I think it's Charlotte," he managed to croak out, "I think she's down there, waiting for me."

Molly swayed as if struck. Her grip on his arm now drew blood, and she closed her eyes tightly as if she could deny this by not seeing it. She tended towards being high strung in the first place, and Bernie found himself wondering if she were about to faint.

"That is insane!" she gritted through clenched teeth, "That woman is dead, and she is not down there waiting for anybody! It's just a sheet, or a tarp that blew off some farmer's trailer when he drove by earlier." Her face started to relax as she reasoned her way to this new conclusion.

Bernie watched her warily as he started to pry her fingers off of his arm. Already frightened himself, the last thing he needed right now would be for her to dissolve into hysterics. Keeping that in mind, he did not point out that her solution required a pole or other object for the "tarp" to catch on...something not to be found out in plowed furrows.

She opened her eyes, and met his with a look of desperate determination.

"It's just a tarp." She repeated. "It's ju... Oh *God*, BERNIE!"

She screamed as she looked towards the field. Bernie floundered to disentangle himself from her retightened grip and turned his head in an effort to see the cause of her outburst. This proved difficult since Molly seemed determined to practically climb on top of him. With an effort, he pushed her away and managed to spot the source of her hysterics.

The figure had moved.

It now appeared, still motionless, in the middle of the plot. Somehow, the apparition had moved halfway across the acreage towards them in the few seconds he took his eyes off of it. Bernie could also make it out better now. He could no longer deny what stood out there in the howling landscape below. It could only be a woman wrapped in loose, dirty white cloth. Thankfully, the failing light and distance combined to obscure the face, but he could now distinguish Charlotte's long, dark hair whipping around against the backdrop of tilled earth

"Oh Lord, Bernie! She's coming for us! We've got to get out of here!"

Bernie continued to stare in numb horror at the wraith waiting down there in the maelstrom, unable to speak. Fear and indecision robbed him of any words. Molly seemed to have no such problem...

"Stay away from me!" she shrieked against the wind, "I didn't *do* anything to you!"

"I don't think she's going to see it that way." Bernie breathed through fear clenched teeth.   After all, Molly had been the "other woman" during the last year of their marriage. Then, when Charlotte found out, that initiated the fight that got her killed.   And it was Molly who rushed over after his despondent phone call, and devised the strategy to cover it up…packing up Charlotte's clothes and toiletries to make it look like she left him. Finally, it was Molly who took it upon herself to throw the first shovelful of dirt into Charlotte's anonymous grave.

No, Bernie felt pretty sure that Charlotte came back to pay both of them a visit.

"This is your fault, Bernie!" Molly screeched. "You got me into this! What are we going to do?"

Surprised, Bernie looked over to see her glaring at him with eyes unnaturally wide, in a face now beyond pale. With her fists clenched by her side, and the cords of her neck sticking out, she looked almost as wild and spectral in the tempest as the approaching horror below. He realized she teetered on the brink of a breakdown.

"Get your stuff!" he shouted back through the wind, "We're getting out of here."   A quick glance back showed the phantom now standing even closer than before. He did not let his gaze linger, not really wanting a better look at it. There are some things in life a man could live without seeing.

Molly floundered her way back towards the house, fighting both the wind and her high heels. Refusing to look back again, Bernie followed as the rain started to fall. It lashed him across the face, forcing him to put up a forearm to shield his eyes. A violent "slam" sounded ahead, as Molly pulled open the screen door and had it ripped out of her hands again by the wind. Cursing viciously, she left it open and staggered into the dark house. He stormed in behind her, his boots thundering on the kitchen floor.

Without power, the inside of the small farmhouse seemed like a murky cave—a cave that creaked and groaned as the winds and rain started to hammer its roof and sides. The shadows of twisting tree limbs played havoc with what little light made it in through the windows.

He could hear Molly pulling out dresser drawers in the bedroom, panting in both panic and exertion. Stumbling down the black hallway, the sound of her frantic preparations gave him a compass he could follow. As he made his way to the bedroom door, a deep hollow spot in his belly told him that none of this would be enough to save them. He could now see her dim figure, grabbing things out of the closet in a desperate frenzy, and stuffing them into her large suitcase.

She stood up to make another dash at the closet, just as nearby lightning illuminated the room with a powerful cracking boom.

Three feet away, Charlotte stared in at her through the window.

Charlotte's time in the black soil of her river bottom grave had not been kind to her looks. There was time for a dirt stained, skullish impression—webbed with small roots and worms—before the flash ended and returned her to a ghastly silhouette against the gloomy outdoors.

Molly's scream was the raw sound of sanity starting to snap.

She somehow managed to stumble, grab her suitcase, right herself, and start running for the door all in one motion. She ran into Bernie, and clawed at him to get past. He caught her by both arms, while still keeping his gaze locked on the wind whipped form at the window.

"Let me go!" she shrieked, losing ground to panic by the second.

"Molly *stop*!" he roared back, tightening his grip. "Listen to me! You have to stay here for a moment!" She fought furiously, making inarticulate noises as she struggled.

He needed to get her to listen. Everything counted on it. He had the germ of a plan, but it all depended on her cooperation.

"Molly!" he shook her, while still watching the window, "You have to stay *here*! I have to go get the car and you need to stay here! She only moves when we take our eyes off of her. I need you to stay here and watch her while I go get the car!"

"No!" Molly screeched, "I'm not going to let you leave me here! I'm going with you!"

"MOLLY!" he thundered, trying to break through her panic by sheer volume. "If you come with me, she'll be waiting for us at the door! Or in the next room! Or in that hallway right there when we turn around! YOU HAVE TO STAY HERE AND WATCH HER!"

For a second, he thought he would need to slap her, but then she quit fighting. Her arms fell limp by her side and she just leaned there against him, not making a sound. He put his hand on her back, fearing she had passed out. Then her shoulders began to shake and she started to cry.

"Bernie," she sobbed, "please don't make me do this."

"You have to, hon," he urged softly. "That way I can make it to the car out in the garage, and then pull it up beside the house. You stay here and keep an eye on her, and then when you hear me honk, you run for the backdoor. I'll keep an

ed himself that if their
roles were reversed, and she could drive a car,
then she would have almost assuredly already
left him.

"Molly," he continued in a gentle tone, "it's
the only way we are going to get out of here. You
have to do this, or she'll get us."

For a moment she did not answer, but then the
sobs started to subside.

When she finally raised her head and looked at
him, he could tell she had now reached the point
where despair became the last refuge of sanity.
She did not trust him, and she did not really
believe he would stop the car and honk, but it
was all the hope left to her. She would do as
told, even though she expected him to leave her
here alone.

Taking her by her small shoulders, he turned
her with care to face the window. Rain now
drummed against it, dimming and blurring the
outline of the horrific thing standing right
outside. Molly's eyes were wide and glassy, and
her breath came in shallow gulps. She fixed her
gaze on the window with an audible whimper.

"Okay," he breathed into her ear, "I'll only
be gone for a couple of minutes. Whatever you
do, do *not* take your eyes off of her. If you do,
she'll be in here with you."

He knew he was pushing too hard, but he needed
her more frightened of looking away than looking
at the thing. He needed her to buy him time.
Having reinforced her fear, he now needed to give
her something to hang on to.

"When you hear me honk the horn," he continued,
"you back out of the room, while still looking

at her. You keep your eye on her for as long as you can, and then you turn and run for the back door. I'll be watching the backdoor so she can't appear there."

Molly only nodded in response, her face so tight he could make out the bones under the skin.

Carefully releasing her shoulders, Bernie backed out of the dark bedroom. He continued backing down the hall, keeping an eye on Molly's small silhouette in the bedroom door. She did not move, although she appeared to tremble once. Once he reached the kitchen, Bernie wheeled and lunged for the back door.

It still hung open from their desperate retreat into the house a few minutes ago, and water blew inside in sheets across the kitchen floor. The storm outside now raged in earnest, trees thrashing in the howling wind. Bernie found stepping out on the back steps to be like stepping into a waterfall…that fell sideways. The sheer volume of water filling the air staggered him as it blew by.

Drenched to his skin in seconds, Bernie reoriented himself and staggered off towards the garage. The short grass of the back yard lay slick with wet, and he fell twice while trying to navigate the distance in the wind. Both times he experienced the stomach wrenching thought he would look up to see Charlotte gazing back down on him. That served to remind him of the fact she stood right around the corner of the house from where he lay. Pushing himself up and forward, he forced his way towards the black outline of the garage.

The '55 station wagon would be parked in there, full of gas. He did not have a lot of use for it on a farm, but Molly insisted he drive her

around town in something other than a farm truck.
So a trip to the used car lot in Hallisboro, and
another note to pay on, got him a second vehicle.
Being newer than the old truck parked behind the
tool shed, he decided the car made the wiser
choice of vehicles in this hurricane.

Bernie staggered through the cascade falling
in front of the open garage door and did a quick
fearful scan of the interior. The rain roaring
against the shingles above drowned out the sigh
of relief he exhaled. Nothing shared the garage
with him but the car.

Moving quickly, he stumbled around to the
driver's side of the car. Another flash of
lightning illuminated the dark, and brought a
scream from the house he could hear over the
storm. If Molly still held the phantom with her
gaze, he doubted it would be for much longer. He
cursed in desperation as he attempted to push his
hand down into his soggy blue jeans pocket to get
the key. He struggled with the sick certainty
that every second he took increased the chance
he would hop into the car only to find the rotting
thing at the window sitting right beside him.

Finally yanking the keys free, Bernie fumbled
with the lock and then jerked the door open.
Caution made him do a quick scan of the car, to
make sure nothing waited for him within. A glance
showed the car remained empty, so he dove inside.
Slamming the door shut, he jammed the key into
the ignition and pumped the gas pedal furiously.

The engine turned, but failed to catch.

Swearing in desperation, Bernie turned the key
again. For a second, the engine turned again,
and then it roared to life. With a shuddering
sigh of relief, he dropped it into gear and
eased out into the storm. Rain smashed into the

windshield, completely obscuring the view. He
turned on the wipers, but they could not even
begin to keep up with the deluge. Switching on
the headlights, he squinted in an effort to make
out the driveway before him.

Due to the direction of the wind, and the
angle of the rain, he could see out the passenger
side window a little better than his windshield.
As he carefully rolled forward, he could see the
dim hulk of the house approach as he started to
come up beside it.

"She's already gone," he muttered, "keep
going." He knew that was exactly what Molly
would do. She would feel terrible about it
later, but would tell herself she had been too
frightened to think. Her "frailties" were often
their own built in excuse. But could *he* do that?

Torn over what to do—keep his promise and
endanger himself further, or run for it and leave
Molly behind—Bernie compromised. He continued
forward at a slow crawl, and started honking the
horn. He needed to give Molly a chance. He just
could not bring himself to stop the car.

Not with Charlotte out there somewhere.

The blurry shape of the house slowly slid by
in the downpour. Twice more, lightning flared—
illuminating both the small farmhouse and the
storm lashing at it. The black windows glared
back at him as if in accusation, showing no hint
of the house's interior. The back door swung
freely, the sound of its slamming penetrating its
way into the car. Bernie leaned on the horn as
he passed, fear crawling up and down his spine.
By the time the car inched its way to the other
end of the house, the gut sinking reality hit
home—Molly would not be coming out.

Bernie refused to think of what could be
happening in there, and turned his attention to

the driveway ahead. What little he could see of it, anyways. His windshield had become a cascade that the wipers only gave brief glimpses through. That, and the deafening pounding of the rain on the car roof, seemed to bury him in the fury of the storm. The lone sound of his own ragged breathing kept him company.

The next swipe of the wipers gave a brief glimpse of asphalt in the headlights. The road now crossed before him. To his left, the tiny town of Weyrich lay about five miles down the road. To his right, Hallisboro offered more substantial civilization about ten miles further. After a brief second's consideration, Bernie turned right.

He hoped that putting the back of the car to the wind would ease the torrent against his windshield and improve visibility. Not to mention, he wanted to surround himself with people right now, and Weyrich offered little more than a wide spot in the road and a store that would be closed. Hallisboro would have emergency shelters open. And people. Wonderful, wonderful crowds of people. He would have to cross the Brazos to get there, but the rain had not been falling long enough to bring the river up yet. He needed to hurry, though.

Thankfully, turning right did ease the assault on his windshield and visibility improved. Not by much, but at least he could see the road fifty feet ahead of him. The storm now closed the world in around the car, crowding close with grey curtains that turned even nearby objects into dim silhouettes. He never felt so alone in his life.

Taking a deep breath, Bernie shifted in his soggy clothes and focused forward. Easing on the gas, he got the car rolling down the hill. He

did not want to allow it to go too fast on the
incline, because brakes could be a catastrophic
choice in this weather even at normal speeds.
This turned out to be a wise precaution, because
he found himself forced to stop just as he reached
the bottom of the hill.

Fifty feet ahead, the specter stood in his
headlights.

Bernie's air simply left him. He could clearly
make out the pale figure in the sodden white dress
through the water distortion on his windshield.
The shape waited in silence, the only sounds
being the raindrops thundering on the car, and
the rhythmic thump of the wipers. He gripped the
steering wheel, his eyes like those of a cornered
animal. There remained one thing to do.

He could not back up, and the road was too
narrow to turn around. Water now cascaded down
the ditches on each side. He could not stay here
staring at the ghost either, because the river
ahead of him would be rising soon, and he now sat
at the bottom of the hill in its flood plain. In
less than an hour, this area would be underwater.
In far less time than that, the bridge ahead
would be impassible. He needed to go.

Now.

Setting his jaw, he narrowed his eyes at the
figure ahead and stepped on the gas. The car
lurched forward and gathered speed. The horrid
figure ahead grew rapidly and filled his headlights.
At the last second, just as the root webbed
visage became clear in his windshield, he threw
up his arm in reflex, anticipating the impact.

It never came.

For a brief moment, elation filled him as he
realized he drove unimpeded down the road towards
the river. Then he realized his fatal mistake as
the smell of rot and black earth filled the car.

He had taken his eyes off of her when he looked away at that last second.

Bernie screamed as two icy cold arms enveloped him from behind, and he reflexively jerked the wheel to the side.

"Hello, baby," Charlotte's dirt choked voice whispered in his ear. "Let's go home."

★★★

Hurricane Carla tore through Texas in early September of 1961, causing catastrophic damage. Due to evacuation procedures, the dead in Texas only came to thirty-one despite the ferocity of the storm.

Molly Johnson did not count against that total since her death was ruled a homicide. Authorities found her body, strangled and wrapped in an old rotted sheet, in the hallway of a small farmhouse owned by Bernard (Bernie) March. They assumed March killed her, and then fled out into the hurricane, only to slide off the road at the Old Weyrich Bridge over the Brazos River. County police discovered his car overturned at the bottom of the bridge.

His body was never found.

About the author:
D. Nathan Hilliard lives in Spring, Texas, with his veterinarian wife, two children, and two cats. He draws his inspiration from a childhood living in different small Texas towns, accented by teen years spent in western New Mexico. He

has experienced life through a diverse collection of jobs ranging from meter reading and being an assistant manager at a convenience store, to working at cotton gins, window factories, and uranium mills. After coming down with Charcot Marie Tooth (CMT) at the turn of the century, Mr. Hilliard now happily settles for tending house, raising his kids, and exploring the field of writing.

Amanda C. Davis

Stills and Rushes

The first time I saw the thing in the creek, I was nine. I barely caught a glimpse of it. It slid like a mossy birch between the roots of a tree growing just at the edge of the creek: fat and greenish, gone in a moment. I threw stones at the pool framed by the tree's roots, but nothing came out again, and I went home disappointed.

The second time, my parents were with me, but they were collecting rusted beer cans into a garbage bag and wouldn't let me help, so neither of them saw the sudden thick bloom of hair trickle from the pool beneath the tree, and neither saw a green fleshy thing slip back into the dark when they pulled me away from the edge.

The third time, my little sister came along. She ran off in tears and I got in trouble for scaring her, and for getting algae stains on my new jeans.

After that, the times ran together: glimpses of green, the sensation of slime sliding past a bare ankle. It was a hot summer. The creek ran cold and the air around the pool always held a chill. I spent a lot of time climbing around wet rocks, trying and failing to skip stones. I caught crayfish, and once, a snail. My fingers grew pale and wrinkled beneath the water, although sometimes when I looked I saw bloated ones, with the sheen of dead fish in green and gray. I made sure to stay away from the deep pools. But I couldn't help staring into their depths.

Late that summer, my parents left us in the care of a neighbor for a week. I don't remember where they went—on business or to escape two demanding little girls—but I do remember that it rained every day but the last. From my bedroom window I could look across the overgrown backyard and just see the white foam of the swollen creek.

On the last day before my parents returned I put on my oldest sneakers and the jeans that still had algae stains.

"Where are you going?" asked the neighbor—she had a frustrating habit of caring where we went.

I told her I was going to play in the creek.

She shook her head and drew me gently back from the door. "Oh no, not today," she said. "The creek's too high for little girls. You know, when I was your age a girl drowned in that creek after a big rain like this. She had pretty long hair like yours. Come on, let's get your sister and go to the playground instead."

I never did see it again. But then, I didn't play in the creek too much for the rest of the summer either. How could I, after finding out about something like that?

About the author:

Amanda C. Davis is a Pittsburgh engineer with a green thumb, a fondness for horror movies, and a habit of constantly gaining new hobbies. As a child she spent a lot of time playing in the creek. She blogs at http://davisac1.livejournal. com.

Alison Seay

A Hopeful Mother

Mallory was born in high summer. With the windows of her nursery thrown open, the cicadas screamed her to sleep every night. She liked spiders when she was old enough to crawl. She brought them to her mother, Bernadette, with frightening regularity. She did not have a name for them until she could talk, and when she could she called them "eightsies" for their eight legs.

"Mallory, they're bugs," Bernadette said. And she shuddered. She knew it was wrong to dissuade her daughter from her natural interests and inclinations, but creepy crawly things freaked her out.

"Actually, mother," Mallory said, "they're arachnids."

Her husband, Jefferson, laughed, and his chest puffed up with pride—a daughter of his correcting his very smart wife about the difference between a bug and an arachnid. He would remind his wife that bugs were normal when you lived the rural life. He found it amusing. Normally, it would have tickled Bernie's funny bone too, but something about Mallory's fascination frightened her. Way down where her maternal instincts lived, she was scared. Was it normal for a girl Mallory's age to always have some bug companion?

She had found crickets in Mallory's overalls and ants in an Altoid tin in her room. They had a leaf in there and crawled around, content in their hinge-lidded microscopic paradise—until Bernie opened the lid and they flowed out like a black speckled dribble of water. She had screamed and dropped the tin, more from surprise than anything else. After all, they were only ants. Mallory had herded them back in the tin and left the room without a word to her mother.

But Bernie heard her talking to the damn ants once she was out in the hall.

Her daughter collected fireflies and set them loose in their house the summer she was six. She would not talk to the neighbor child and had no friends in school, but she talked to lightning bugs and katydids. Bernie grew more worried. More scared. God help her—more ashamed. Her daughter was clearly off. What did that say about her?

Later that summer, Mallory brought a bucket of crickets inside and set them free in her room. "To bring the outside inside," Mallory said. She liked the sound and wanted to feel close to the bugs. Bernie spent weeks with her Dyson vacuum trying to suck them up. A few managed to get away and they would hear random chirping throughout the house. Eerily, Mallory could always locate and lure the rebel chirpers.

It was the box of maggots that did Bernie in. The bug that broke the mother's back, so to speak. One chicken bone, one shoe box, one funky smell and a writhing mass of white bugs that looked like dingy animate Tic-Tacs. Bernie promptly threw up and put her foot down.

"All bugs out," she said, and emptied the house of every ant farm and rogue cricket. Those odd sprickets in the basement got sprayed with hairspray so they were immobilized, and then stomped. The two pet spider webs that hung in

Mallory's otherwise unused closet were torn down. The wasp nest on the front porch was burned, as was the hornet's nest out by the shed.

All the while Jefferson tried to "talk some sense" into her and let Mallory have her childhood interests. Mallory watched with big, empty, blowfly green eyes—silent and hollow as her mother tore through her carefully built insect community.

***

Bernadette felt someone standing there. At first she thought it was Jefferson, but then she remembered that he was in Memphis for a sales convention. She was nearly alone on the old homestead while Jefferson traveled.

That meant it was Mallory.

Bernie steeled herself. She wanted to lie in the sun in the hammock, the book she was supposed to be reading shielding her eyes from the early afternoon sun. She did not want to deal with her daughter. She did not want to argue over refusing to buy a tarantula or purchasing a new ant farm. She simply could not deal with another conversation about maybe finding some rare moths available online. People spent tons of money to protect their houses and clothing from moths, why in the world would she spend hard earned money to actually purchase them?

"Please, Mallory," she said. She did not even cover her eyes. "Please, no more fighting. Mommy simply cannot do it."

She waited and all she heard was the soft, barely audible sound of barefeet on fresh green grass, and soft breathing. Her daughter was there, pouting, giving her mother the cold shoulder.

And that was fine, Bernie decided, as long as the cold shoulder was insect-free.

It startled her when a small, smooth hand slid into her own and squeezed. Bernie pulled the book from her eyes and stared at her daughter. Mallory was not what one would call a naturally affectionate child. Oh, sure, she'd stroke the shit out of an earthworm or pet a centipede, but humans? Not so much.

"Mal?"

"Will you take a walk with me, Mommy? Annie and her mom go on hikes. Maybe we could hike, too. And then have a picnic?"

Bernie's heart contracted in her chest. A mix of fear, excitement, and yes, hope.

"We can," she stammered. "Sure we can, honey. Let me get my shoes and put on bug spray."

Mallory shook her head. "That stuff is poison. Daddy says so. You just need your shoes."

Bernie figured they could walk the old trail that wound through a small wooded area nearby. The opening to the scarcely used trail was just up the road from them. They could walk and return home for a picnic with lemonade and the watermelon she had bought the day before at the Peterson's roadside stand. The woods were relatively small and surrounded by nothing but flat green landscape. They could have peanut butter and jelly sandwiches and animal crackers and talk about the upcoming school year and what color Mallory would paint her room for her next birthday. Anything to get rid of the pill bug slate color she chose a few years back. And they could...bond.

Bernie was heartened that tough love finally seemed to be working.

"Ready, mommy?" Mallory stood there smiling.

Smiling!

When was the last time she had seen anything beyond a secretive, dreamy half-smile on Mal's face? Bernie could not remember.

"I'm almost ready. Did you want to ask Annie and her mom?" Once she had put a ban on bugs, Mallory had occasionally gone to play up the road with a little girl her age. Annie's was the only house for a few miles, and lived not far from the trail. This is probably how the idea of a hike had gotten in Mallory's head. Either way, Bernadette was grateful. Maybe if they invited Annie and her mom, she too could make a friend in the neighborhood and they could have fantastic mother daughter days. Outings to town. Movies and shopping and lunch. All the things she dreamed of when she imagined having a daughter.

"No. Just us, okay? Special. We will have a special day together."

Bernie felt a brief but severe white stab of doubt. She soldiered past her internal warning and smiled. "Great. Just me and you, kiddo. We'll hike and maybe find a secret grotto or a river or a jungle or a time warp back in time!" she joked. It felt forced and foreign but Bernie did it anyhow.

"Maybe," Mallory said and smiled her newly grown enthusiastic smile again.

It was high summer and hot as an oven in Hell but Bernie got a chill. She shook it off and stood, reaching for the bug spray but catching herself. "Oops. We'll go au natural. Let's go."

They grabbed their water bottles and off they went.

Halfway up the long road, they approached Annie's house. The house sat back from on road.

Recessed by a lush front lawn sat a big white
farm house. "Last chance. Are you sure you don't
want to invite Annie and her mom?"

Mallory nodded. "I'm sure. This way." She put
her hand in her mother's again and poor Bernadette
blushed deeply, feeling a tug so urgent she swore
it reached her womb.

"All right then. Just us girls." Her voice
was clogged with unshed tears and she swallowed
hard to keep them that way. "Let's go."

The woods were dense, the path barely visible.
Very few people used it. Bernadette watched for
holes and pits in the trail. As a young girl,
she had stepped in a rabbit hole and broken
her ankle. The memory of having her throbbing
wounded ankle stuck in that hole never seemed to
fade when she was faced with nature. She had
never felt more hopeless (and had not since)
than being pinned there until her father could
help disengage her swiftly swelling appendage.
Bernadette remembered the sharp and cloying panic
that flared in her chest at having part of her
trapped below ground, in the dark. Who knew what
was down there.

Bernadette stumbled on a rock and yelped,
shaken from her reverie. Mallory walked a few
steps head, her migration tried and true as if she
had traveled the path a million times already.
"You sure know your way around," she joked.

"I just listen," Mallory said and she shut her
eyes. Her head tilted back and she seemed to
sway a bit as if keeping beat with some unheard
music. All Bernie could hear was the screeching,
shrill sound of the cicadas and the drone of
the rest of the woods. The whole of it seemed
alive.

Bernie noticed the apprehension a second time.
The feel of the woods pressing in on her—like

it was hungry and she was fair game. She shook her head and smiled at herself. It was just a nice case of the heebie jeebies. Her husband was away, her daughter was just starting to act like a person and not the world's creepiest beekeeper, and she was trying to find some common ground with Mallory. It would all work out.

She slipped again, this time on something cool and damp. It smeared over the rock she had stepped on, a grayish brown blob of gelatinous something.

"Are you okay, mommy?" Mallory asked. She put her hand on Bernie's arm in a comforting gesture, but her skin was too cool. It looked fine but felt a bit too moist. Bernie noticed that Mallory rocked her head in a monotonous motion, reminding Bernie of a centipede reared up on its back legs, head and forelimbs swaying to gain it's bearings.

"Fine! I'm fine, babe!" Bernie said it a bit too loud, a bit too high. Mallory threw her a knowing smile—a malicious expression.

"Good. Come on, mommy. There's so much to show you."

"So you have been here."

"Of course. I have hiked and played and hunted and gathered."

"You and Annie?"

"Me, mostly."

Now she was skipping.

Big, leaping girly skips up the narrow shamble of a path.

Bernie squinted. *Stared.* Shook her head.

Mallory seemed to be gaining too much air, getting way too high off the ground for mere skips. Bernadette wiped her eyes with her forearm. Maybe she had too much sun.

"Well, I'm glad you know your way, otherwise I'd worry!"

Again her voice was too high and too thin, but she was not sure how to stop it, so she did nothing. Bernie plodded on, the pit of her stomach buzzing with nerves, her head throbbing, her knees aching. Her ankle hurt a bit, the one she had broken so long ago, from her stumble on the rocks.

Maybe this had been a bad idea. They had not even told anyone where they were going. What if something happened? What if she became sick or passed out? What then? What would Mallory do?

Panic flared in her.

"Wait until you see, mommy. The place that Annie and I found. Our place!" Mallory tossed the words over her shoulder like summer flowers as she ran. Bernie had to hustle to keep up and her ankle protested with little stabs of pain.

"Mal, wait. Maybe it's not safe for you to rush ahead of mommy." She worried something would happen and swore she could feel the dense canopy of vibrant green trees lean in to watch her move like an ant in a jar. "Wait for mommy, Mal."

Don't leave me here. I'm scared.

It felt like another planet as opposed to less than a third of a mile from her safe, familiar home.

"Just a bit more, mommy!" Mallory crowed. Bernie turned the corner, hit a hole and went down. Her foot twisted and then sank, and she screamed out before she could stop herself, clawing at the air and the shoddy bark of a young sapling. "Oh, mommy. Are you fine?"

There was a smile in the girl's voice.

Are you fine? An odd "Mallorism", as she and Jefferson called them. The girl had a clipped and foreign way of talking at times, sometimes substituting strange sounds for words she could not seem to pluck from her head.

For oven she made a soft hissing sound like something roasting in heat.

A high keening sound would come from her when she was anxious. It would issue from deep in the child's chest with a piercing whistle. The sound of Mallory in distress could set teeth on edge.

She said *are you fine?* as opposed to *are you okay?*

She said *I can do this, yes?*

Too many stilted ways of speaking that made them wonder. But every doctor said she was fine—a healthy normal young girl who just had her own specific ways.

Mallory's eyes shone with a multifaceted glee as she crept in toward Bernadette to examine her. Bernie felt like a butterfly pinned to a board.

"Help me, Mallory," she snapped. She used her best brave voice and put a lot of no-nonsense mom courage in it. She put her hand up and said, "Come on. Now, Mallory, don't dawdle."

"Will you be nice?" Mallory leaned over her, her mouth working for no apparent reason—talking to something or someone that Bernie couldn't see.

"What? Yes! Yes, I will be very nice, Mallory. Now help me. My foot is swelling."

Mallory pulled at Bernie's arm and slowly they managed, together, to get Bernadette up and free.

Had she told the story of the injured ankle? And if she had, had Mallory somehow managed to… No. That was nuts.

It was a small wooden shack that Mallory wanted to show and Bernadette stifled her arguments and went. The smell hit her in the face when the door was thrown wide, but it was too dark to see.

"My god. What is that? You and Annie have been playing here? That's not safe," she started, but then Mallory ducked around her and darted into the gloom. She tugged Bernie hard enough to make her stumble.

The pale slumped figure in the corner did not register at first. A small humanoid that seemed to be sparkling, shifting, roiling. Mallory made a series of odd clicks and moans in her throat and then turned to Bernie and smiled. "They're glad you're here."

"They're?"

It was when she leaned in and really squinted that she saw the shape was a person.

A small person.

Not roiling or shifting, but teeming with maggots. The figure seemed alive—and in some aspects, *was* alive—with the clamoring, squishy white bodies.

Bernie could not manage a scream. She swallowed it, clamping her hand over her mouth, eyes wide. Mallory grinned. "Annie was fun, but they needed her more than I did."

Jesus Christ. "They?" Bernie said through slit fingers.

"Them." Mallory indicated the maggots, then dipped her head to the floor. "And them."

Spiders. Ants. Centipedes. The floor moved around her feet like the ocean sucking the tide back out from the shore.

An itch started between her eyebrows and shoulder blades. A bone deep shiver rustled along her spine. Bernadette observed somewhat clinically that she was too terrified to make much noise.

What did that mean when you were so scared you basically observe yourself?

"Oh, Mallory."

The bug ban had driven her to build a little getaway—the insect version of a love shack.

Bernie's head felt too light, not tethered to her neck. Her ears rang higher and sharper than any cicada song.

"Have a seat, mommy," the girl said.

Bernie turned. She caught the blow from the small piece of wood in the face—not hard enough to crack her teeth or break her nose—just hard enough to make shining stars of light around her head. Bernadette inadvertently complied by folding in on herself like a lawn chair and landing in the seat next to the wriggling white mass. The smell alone triggered her gag reflex but she was too stunned to react.

"Mallory, please." Bernadette still allowed herself some hope that this was a mistake, a joke…an illusion.

She saw the wood coming at her again, but her reflexes were too far gone to be triggered in time. The piece of wood hit her broadside to the temple and sparks of fire popped in her vision. Bernadette moaned. She shook her head in denial but the world was already moving, and that motion just made it worse. Her stomach spiraled with nausea. "Mallory."

"Shh. I can't hear them if you keep talking." Mallory laughed softly and that sound was nothing like the laughter of a child that mothers around the world cherish. That sound made Bernadette's heart stutter in her chest.

She noticed a larger humped shape in an old camping chair.

It sat lumpy and gauzy in the far corner. Bernadette knew it was not gauze—it was webbing.

Annie's mother, Claire.

Again, the scream died in her throat. She was too damn tired to scream. Mallory's head tilted back, swaying to her alien symphony, moving the small wooden board like a baton. She had never been right. Never fit in. Bernadette swallowed the gorge that rose in her throat. She did not beg any more.

The first of the troop tickled at her throbbing ankle.

Something slithered up her leg.

Do not look. She was too far outnumbered to fight. She saw that now. The windows were boarded up, but around the cracks marched tidy single-minded lines of ants and silverfish.

"Would you like me to stay with you or leave?" Mallory asked with her eyes closed. "They don't care much about that stuff."

"Let me go."

Hope.

"No."

"Leave, then."

She watched her daughter turn—her odd smooth skin, her high strange noises, her shiny faceted green eyes, her invisible tether to another kingdom.

Mallory did not tie her or hit her again. She had too much faith in her skittering kin to worry about her mother escaping. Bernadette heard the door lock from the outside. She listened to the whispers of the multitudes on the dry rotted wood of the shack, on her skin.

She wondered if she should have kept her daughter here with her. *It would be better easier to die with her gone*.

About the author:

Alison Seay writes full-time as many different people. Once in a while she writes as herself. This is one of those instances. She can be reached at www.alisonseay.wordpress.com

Rob Rosen

Closer by the Second

Titus Rawlings rolled along in his dusty, old covered wagon and gave a great holler. "Look wife, we's here!"

"Again?" his wife, Myrna, replied, deep from within the wagon. "Where we at this time?"

"Somewhere in Okleehomee, I reckon."

He was, of course, correct, for that was where they were headed. Congress had passed a bill three years prior allowing for homestead settlements in what was previously Indian Territory. Titus and his wife had left Chicago a year earlier, and had already traveled through Iowa, Nebraska, and Kansas in search of a few good acres of land to start a farm on, to call home. Unfortunately, there was none to be had, least none worth having. The West, it seemed, had opened up and then rapidly filled.

"Okleehomee?" Myrna sighed, peeking her head out from a side flap. "Where in tarnations is that?"

Titus scratched his balding scalp, and replied, "West of Arkansas and north of Texas, I reckon. And look, wife, there's land as far as the eye can see."

His wife did indeed look, and she was none too happy with what she saw.

"You call this land?" Myrna asked, with a frown on her furrowed face. "Looks like desert to me."

Oklahoma had been known as the Great American Desert, which was why the U.S. Government created the Indian Territory there in the first place—as a home for all the Indian tribes. Why give them land that anybody would want?

But Titus was desperate. And dirt poor. Dirt everything, actually. They and all their worldly possessions were fairly covered in it. "Now wife," he tried, with a forced smile, "I wouldn't call it desert, really. I think they call this part we's approaching prairie land. From what I been told, we can grow corn, wheat, and oats out here once we find ourselves a lake or a stream or something."

"We should've stayed in Chicago," she snapped. "Least we could shop for clothes and food, and could take a bath once in a while."

He had heard this argument for the last several hundred miles. And there were quite a few times he thought about ditching his ornery wife by the side of what little road there was, but then who would help him set up the farm? Besides, as he had told her, life in Chicago was not any better. Work was scarce, and food and clothes were expensive, at least by his standards, which were low at best.

"Well now, wife, let's give it a chance. Chicago can be our second option." The wagon continued onwards.

She harrumphed and stuck her head back inside. "You was *my* second option, Titus. I shoulda married that there carpenter feller, Otis Elwood," she said from the back.

"Lucky Otis Elwood," Titus replied, under his breath.

"What was that?" she screamed at him.

"I said, lucky us, there's a stream up ahead."

And that there was—a winding blue stream that parted the scrubby land and allowed for a few short trees here and there. It was a veritable green oasis out in the middle of nowhere. Something, however, seemed off.

"Strange," Titus said to himself. "No homes or farms out here. No town. No nothing. And it's silent as a whisper." He chalked it up to the remoteness of the place, and then stopped the wagon and hopped off. "Lucky for us," he added, yet again.

"Not so lucky," came a deep, grumbling voice from behind him.

Titus jumped and tripped over a rock. "What in tarnation?" he shouted as he rubbed a scraped elbow.

"Close," the stranger said. "So close."

"Close to what?" Titus asked. He squinted and held his hands up to shade his eyes. The sun had risen directly behind the stranger, and the corona around his head was blinding poor Titus something fierce.

"Close to hell," the man said with a hearty chuckle.

Titus rubbed the tears from his watery eyes, and asked, "Where'd you come from, stranger? And what in blazes are you talking about?"

"Names Jeb Malloy. And this here's my land. Well, used to be, anyhows."

"Used to be? I don't see no homes here. No farms. No people. Where'd you live if this was, as you say, *your* land?"

Jeb Malloy gave no reply. He shook his head and grinned at the still-stunned Titus. Eventually, he broke the silence with, "This here's Injun burial land, partner. Choctaw Injuns, to be exact."

"So these Injuns own the land?" Titus had never met a real life Indian before. He was nervous and equally excited at the prospect.

"Nope, ain't no one *owns* it. It's just theirs."

"And that's why there's no farms or people around?"

"That's one reason," Jeb responded, cryptically.

"So, legally, I could set up home here, right?" There was hope in Titus's voice.

"Legally? Well yes, I reckon. But the Injuns might have something to say about that." Again he laughed a big belly laugh that caused Titus to nervously wriggle and wince. It was a laugh that rattled poor Titus to the quick.

"What Injuns?" he thought to ask. "There ain't nobody around here. I ain't seen hide nor hair of anybody since we left Kansas.

Jeb Malloy leaned in close, until they were eye to bloodshot eye. The laughter had ceased, and a terrifying frown spread across the stranger's wizened face. "Oh, they's around, partner. They's around, all right." And with that, Jeb quickly moved his head to the right, so that Titus was now looking directly into the sun. Titus's hands shot to his face, and he rubbed frantically at his burning eyes.

"Where?" he shouted at the stranger, in a fit of blindness. "Where are they?"

There was, however, no response.

"Jeb?" Titus yelled. "Please tell me, where are they?"

Still there was silence, save for the rustling of the wind and the tinkling of the stream.

Titus managed to squint his eyes open. When he was again able to focus, he found that Jeb was no longer there.

"Where's who?" his wife asked, emerging from the wagon. "And who were you talking to just now?"

"Didn't you see him, wife?"

"See who, you crazy coot?"

Titus looked forward and then back, but they were alone. "Never mind, wife. Must've been the sun playing tricks on me." He stood up and got his bearings. He was shaken, but tried his darndest not to show it. Myrna just stood there with her arms akimbo and a miserable glower spreading on her sun-baked face.

She spit on the ground, and said, "My mama warned me about marrying you, Titus." And then she hopped back inside the wagon.

"Well, how come nobody warned me?" Titus mumbled.

"What was that?" she screamed.

"I said, warm the fire and set up the tent, wife." Once again, Titus looked around the area. He looked in front and behind him, and then up and down the stream. He even looked under the damn wagon, but there was no Jeb Malloy to be found. "Stupid midday heat," he grumbled, and then tried his hardest to forget the encounter entirely.

In fact, he tried the whole time they were pitching camp, tried the whole time he was eating his meager dinner—and tried while he and his wife lay in their tent after a long, hard day of work. He tried and failed miserably. "Where on earth did that man disappear to, and what was he yammering on about?" he asked himself as his wife snored loudly by his side.

There was no answer, but in the distance, through the sound of the howling wind, he could swear he heard that big, raucous laugh of Jeb's, and then the words, "Close. So close."

Titus trembled and scrunched his body up tight beneath the blanket. Sleep was not to come to him that night.

He rose the next morning, groggy and unsure of his decision to stay. He looked around his camp in the bright light of day. Again, something was not quite right. He could not put his finger on it, but the place was not like it should have been.

Then he recalled the hours of endless travel to get to this destination, the fruitless excursions from one town to the next, and he thought of the hours he would have to travel to get back, with his wife cursing his very existence the entire time, and he decided once again to settle on the spot he had chosen—Jeb Malloy or no Jeb Malloy, Indians or no Indians.

"Wife," he said, after a disappointingly sparse breakfast, "I'm gonna go search for a nearby town. We'll need to buy our seeds and wares from somewhere eventually."

Myrna eyed him meanly and said nothing.

Titus turned away from her and hopped on one of his horses. When he was a few feet away from their camp, he added, "And maybe find me a nice whore while I'm at it."

"What did you say?" his wife shouted.

"I said, finish your chores while I'm away." He waved with his back to her and followed the stream, figuring it would lead to a town.

What it led to, much to his dismay, was Jeb Malloy.

"You again?" Titus said as he rode up alongside the man. Jeb was sitting by the stream, his pant legs rolled up and his feet dangling in the crystal clear water.

"You still hangin' 'round here?" Jeb responded with a question of his own, the impish grin reappearing on his leathery face.

"Yep," Titus replied. "Gonna start me a farm on that land back there. Maybe grow some corn. Get me some cattle down the line, too."

"But I done warned you already, that's Injun burial land."

"Then they won't be any the wiser, will they? Besides, it ain't their land no more. The government done opened it up."

Jeb jumped up and cast Titus a wicked sneer. "Now, partner, this land is always their land. Always has been, always will be. It don't matter if the government says so or not."

"Then how come you put down roots around these parts?" Titus didn't like this man. No sir, no how. Not one bit.

"Well now, let's just say that I learned my lesson the hard way. Now if you don't mind, I think I'll take me a dip."

"Suit yourself," Titus said. "It's a free country."

"For some it seems to be," Jeb said with his signature laugh, and then he dove up and out, landing in the stream without so much as a splash.

Titus waited for him to reemerge, to ask him where the nearest town was, to ask him where the Indians were, but Jeb never surfaced. Titus rode his horse up and down the side of the stream, but as before, Jeb had vanished.

"Dag nab it," Titus finally said, in desperation. "I betcha he wants the land for himself, is all, and he's trying to scare me off." He shouted into the air with clenched fists raised high, "Well, I ain't leavin'!"

The wind whispered in response, "Close. So close."

A chill ran from the tippy top of Titus's head down to his booted feet. "What's close?" he yelled. "What?"

But there was no answer. Titus turned back around and headed home, afraid of running into Jeb yet again.

"Back so soon?" his wife asked upon his approach.

"Um, yep. The horse got spooked. Besides, there's plenty of work to get done around here first. I'll find us a town once we get set up."

His wife did not say a word. Instead, she stared straight ahead, just over Titus's shoulder, her eyes wide as can be. A lone bead of sweat trickled down her brow. Slowly, Titus turned around to see what she was gaping at. His eyes scanned over and then up. And that is when he spotted them. His stomach dropped to the ground and his heart skipped a beat.

"Injuns," he whispered.

"Injuns," Myrna echoed.

Twenty Indians, to be exact, in full regalia. Each had on dusty, old buckskins and massive feathered headdresses. Even from a distance, Titus could see the streaks of paint on their dark faces and the blacks of their eyes.

Jeb Malloy was leading them down the hill. It was a frightening looking posse. They walked slow and with purpose. When they finally reached the terrified husband and wife, Jeb nodded and snickered at them. The Indians remained stock-still and mute, like the carved, wooden sculpture Titus had seen outside a barbershop when he was a kid.

"Last time I'm gonna ask this, partner—you still planning on staying here?" Jeb asked with an odd smile stretched across his face, like he knew the answer before he even asked the question.

Titus stood his ground. "Yep. I reckon I am," he replied. "There's plenty of land 'round here, and I think we can all live peaceably together on it."

"Live?" Jeb asked, and then broke into howls of laughter.

"What's so funny?" Titus asked with a nervous tic that quivered just above his eyebrow, a feeling of dread pervading his soul.

"Because, partner, there ain't no livin' 'round here. Open your eyes and look around. There ain't no people. No animals. No fish. No birds. No *life*."

Myrna reached out and held on to her husband's hand with a grip of iron. They were both trembling now. "But you. *Them*," he tried.

"Dead," he said, pointing to himself. "And just as dead," he added, pointing to the silent mob behind him.

"Sacred Injun burial land," Titus muttered.

The couple sank to their knees.

"Sacred?" Jeb laughed. "Partner, you are a funny one. I'm glad for that. It gets plumb lonely 'round these parts. You see, I don't speak no Choctaw, and they don't speak no English. Anyways, this ain't no sacred burial land, friend. The Choctaw people were moved from Mississippi to this here Indian Territory by the government more than sixty years ago. This group here, far as I can tell, was the worst of the worst. Criminals, even among their own kind."

"Criminals?" Titus asked, barely above a whisper.

"Oh yeah, a mean lot. Evil. I'm afraid you picked the wrong land to settle on, partner. Just like I did. 'Cause it ain't sacred. Not by a long shot. It's cursed with a powerful magic. And that hell you mentioned, why, you's standin' directly above it."

"Close. So close," Titus spoke, finally getting it.

Jeb laughed long and hard. "Oh, friend, you have no idea."

And then, one by one, the Indians sank into the ground they had been buried in, and down further than anyone could ever have imagined. "Welcome to the Wild West, partner," Jeb said as he, too, started to sink. "Only it's a *hell* of a lot further south than you'da thunk."

Titus and Myrna followed right behind him. Then, quick as wink, the desolate landscape was again bathed in utter silence, save for a strange, ominous laugh, and then an almost imperceptible, "Close now, partner. And getting closer by the second."

About the author:

Rob Rosen, author of the novels "Sparkle" and "Divas Las Vegas", has had short stories featured in more than sixty anthologies, most notably: Short Attention Span Mysteries; Modern Witches, Wizards, and Magic; Southern Comfort; Hell's Hangmen: Horror in the Old West; By the Chimney With Care; Our Shadows Speak; Strange Stories of Sand and Sea; Damned in Dixie: Southern Horror; Sporty Spec: Games of the Fantastic; Legends and Fables: A Fantasy Anthology; Twisted Fayrie Tales; Ruins Metropolis; Don't Turn the Lights On; Speculative Realms; Bloody October; Abaculus 2008; and Black Box. Please visit him at his website, www.therobrosen.com, or email him at robrosen@therobrosen.com

J. Troy Seate

Not Alone

She was alone in the big house. It was late and her mom was not home from her town meeting. She hummed to drown out the occasional creak and groan, tried to convince herself the sounds were merely those of ancient wood and brick settling around her.

Then she heard them coming…slowly…closer… coming up the sidewalk toward the front porch. Muffled voices and shoe heels clattered on the flagstone as they climbed the steps and crossed the porch to her front door.

"Oh, God!" Margaret breathed. She glanced at the solid oak door. It stood ajar for her mother, the entrance blocked only by the fragile screen door, secured with a small hook.

She raced to shut and lock the massive door before they broke down the screen. Before they flooded in and descended upon her.

"No!" she screamed as the screen door ripped away, torn from its hinges. Margaret pushed on the heavy, carved door with all her strength, pushed against the oncoming horde. She slammed her body against it as hard as she could, pushing desperately as gnarled, twisted fingers curled around its edges. She could not stop them. Could not escape. Trapped.

A bony hand grasped her shoulder. Another reached in and wrapped around her neck…and squeezed.

* * *

She awoke so abruptly that she heard the broken-off ending of her own muffled cry. Her head spun. She was exhausted from fighting a gruesome enemy in her last terrifying stages of desolation. *This time they had almost gotten in.* Her heart pounded—the end of the dream holding onto her, still vivid and terrifying.

How odd, Margaret thought. At the age of thirty, this childhood dream returned to torment her so soon after her mother's passing. *She was not there to protect you in your dream, and she is not here now...and she will not be, ever again.*

The air around her was as still as an indrawn breath. Then, she heard a quiet murmur from somewhere in the house. A cold shadow arose in the chambers of her heart. She tried to tell herself the nightmare had triggered her overactive imagination. She wanted to pull the covers over her face like the little girl lost in her, lest she see shadows of the beckoning, clickity-clack skeletons entering her room.

She felt so alone. For years she had awoken to the sounds of her mother padding around the kitchen in the early morning. Those sounds might have comforted Margaret. It might have told her that somehow there was a kindred spirit about and she was not really alone, as if a door to the past might still be open.

Her ears picked up another sound so slight it was barely there at all. It sounded like… snickering. It brought a buried memory to the surface so profound that, for a moment, she was back in the little country school yard.

"Scaredy-cat, scaredy-cat," kids were calling her. It was a childhood chant from a time when she was afraid to retrieve a ball which had rolled into the bushes. She had been positive she saw an emaciated arm hiding among the leaves, waiting to grab the hand of the child who came for the ball. The scene was as vivid today as it had been when she was eight. *Scaredy-cat. Scaredy-cat.* Just a limb with the light hitting it just right, no doubt, but she had run away in tears.

Your mom was not there to protect you then, and she is not here to protect you now.

Margaret fought back fresh tears from the memory, but this was no time for weeping. "When strange shapes appear in obscure corners, a little worm crawls into your brain and makes you believe in things which aren't really there," her mother had assured her when she was little. But it had not kept the skeleton dreams away. And now they had returned, and she was as big a scaredy-cat as ever, with no mother to console her.

Another resonant sound. Something creepily rustling. Not a sound caused by the usual suspects—an old house settling, an attic mouse at play, a breeze whispering through a crack in a window.

Being frightened embarrassed her. Even as a teenager she believed something was trying to get in on those nights when her mother was out late and she was alone until she heard the distinct sound of her mother's shoe-heels on the landing.

As she grew older, she became calmer about such things, although never completely at ease, even as an adult. When her mother got sick and died, she was completely alone for the first time in the old house her long dead grandfather had built. It was so far from the nearest town that the long bus rides which took her to school, and later, the uncommon trips for supplies, added to the feelings of isolation.

But she had always had her mother. All those years, rattling around in the big house, just the two of them. Always the two of them. Until she left, too.

But something else seemed to be rattling around. In the wake of this time of adjustment, the old dream. And sounds were different. This haunting reverie would soon result in a veil of tears for her departed mom if she did not nip her malaise in the bud.

Another snicker—no loitering product of the terrible dream—but something tangible.

She forced herself to sit up and listen, taking in slow, quiet breaths. Floorboards groan and old pipes rattle. Creaks and tappings were normal, but not the hint of voices. She swung her legs off the side of the bed and sat on the edge and listened.

Silence.

It now seemed too quiet, worse than the murmuring and laughing sounds. The unnerving sense of apprehension was worse than the lingering nightmare. She slid unsteadily out of bed. And as ridiculous as she knew it to be, she walked on tiptoes so the sound from sprung floorboards would be less noisy.

Margaret unlocked her bedroom door as quietly as possible. She shivered at the threshold as she peered out beyond the relative safety of her cocoon. The hallway felt colder than usual, an icy zephyr enfolding her body. She could feel the foreboding stir of it in her hair. The light from her bedroom window cast her shadow across the corridor to the opposing wall, stretching it out like the eerie residue of some former inhabitant.

No further acoustics.   It was as if whatever
had caused the sounds was now listening for her.
*What if it is an intruder?   Anyone else is so
far away.   The cleaning lady does not come until
next week.*

She conquered her reluctance to move and
walked to the head of the stairway.   She peered
into the cavernous living room.   A dusky haze of
morning light filtered through the shutters.   She
wondered if someone or some*thing* could be hiding
along a wall, just out of sight—some giggling
thing which would grab hold of her ankle when the
time was right.

She descended the staircase, trying to be as
quiet as a cat on pillows, but floorboards settled
by time made that impossible.   Every hesitant
footfall announced her approach.   She shivered
again with the fear of a waking dream which
might bring her face to face with those terrible
clackity things.

Nothing seemed out of place. But still, she had
heard the sounds—the sigh and the faint chuckle
and the rustling.   There were times when her old
house felt *organic*, like something malevolent,
and this was one of them.

Through the dim light, she saw the door between
the living room and dining rooms slowly draw
shut.   She felt a cold spot where her heart was
supposed to be.   Dark secrets seemed to cling
from every rafter.

*Stop it.   It is an old, creaky house full of
warped wood.*   The doors in the house oftentimes
had lives of their own, but she would not be able
to relax until she made a thorough sweep of the
place.

She sought an adrenalin rush that would give
her the courage to explore.   It did not come,
but the dreaded rounds began nonetheless.   She

reluctantly let go of the stair-knoll and padded through the living room, moving quickly to the oak door from her nightmare.   She checked its locks. *But what good was that if something was already inside?* She walked on to the parlor, the dining room, and through to the kitchen.   Every door was bolted, every window closed and locked. *That was not so bad,* she told herself.

Feeling better, Margaret repeated the journey up the stairs.

But then another sound.   Had she heard the sigh again? A whisper? A brief scuttling sound? A hangover from the nightmare?

Scaredy-cat, scaredy-cat.

Or was it just her imagination carrying her further into a state of delusion that knotted the pit of her stomach?   She listened intently. Seconds passed.   Then a rattle-free minute.

Just old pipes stirring in the walls.

One more room—her mother's.   It was down the hallway from her room.   She did not go in very often.   It brought back sad memories of her mother's illness which simply refused to leave her memory once ensconced therein, but she would not be able to relax until the room-check was complete.   She turned the doorknob and opened the door.   The air thickened and she felt the chill of a room opposite the morning sun.

Then she spied something.   A spider scuttled out from behind her mother's bureau.   And it was not itsy-bitsy.   It scrambled up the wall, making it all the way to the ceiling, where it played possum.   So she was not entirely alone after all.

She hurried to the windows making sure they were closed.   On the outer windowsill, a fallen leaf was snagged.   It was brown and curled upon itself.   It could have been a crunchy, dead spider instead of the live one which kept her company. The gnarled leaf gave her another chill, reminding her of a bony, closed hand. She thought of a spider's web and how fear had so easily drawn her into the sticky threads spun from her nightmare.

A quick look out the window across the rural landscape reminded her of how isolated she was. She quickly turned to leave the room, then froze. A dark silhouette stood before her. She reached for the hollow of her neck to stifle a scream. Her heart slammed against her chest in a moment of panic.

Then she saw the image for what it was—her own reflection in her mom's mirror. She stared stupidly at nothing more than her image and the room reflected back faithfully in its confines, allowing her heartbeat to return to normal. *How pathetic I look in my nightgown, skulking through my own house looking for the skeletons at the door, the one who broke through the barrier of a nightmare and hid in my home!*

She sighed. It was quiet now except for the sound of her breath. She considered a search of the attic. It was undoubtedly decorated with cobwebs and shadows and maybe a city mouse or two. No, she had done enough. She was cold like the house, but that was nothing new. It was old and drafty. She rubbed her hands up and down her arms to remove the chill. A nice, hot shower was in order.

She left her mother's room, her shadow following behind, and shuffled safely back to her own bedroom. But even then, a nagging unease persisted. Living alone could do these kinds of things to a mind—makes a person imagine things beyond their dreams. Giving into the horrors of the imagination was not a remedy for what ailed her. It was a problem she needed to lick now more than ever. If she was going to manage alone, she had to get past her loss, and quickly.

Her mother and she had weathered many storms together, and losing her had been devastating. But Margaret was no longer a child. She could not let these frightening images become like maggots eating away at her thoughts. She must learn to handle any difficulties the world might throw at her. At least in the living, animate world. Her fear was irrational, the product of a too-fertile imagination.

The early morning chill finally sent both the nightmare and the uneasiness skittering back to a more remote corner of her subconscious. She walked toward the adjoining bathroom for her morning shower. She reached into the darkness to turn on the light, bracing herself in the event the nightmare was not completely over, in case something cold and slimy should reach back.

The only sound from her bathroom was the usual *plink* of another water drop in the washbasin. Safe again. Nothing to be afraid of. Nothing at all. No more scaredy-cat. The dream which held a specter of doom fell away completely in the bright light of the little room taking her creepy, cadaverous thoughts with it. Removing her gown, she entered the bathroom. "Silly nightmares," she sighed. Her recovery from her mother's death had already cost too much time in what should be her best years. "Time to get back to reality."

Looking in the mirror and ruffling her hair, she was further calmed by her opaque, powder-blue shower curtain where passive swans glided languidly across its surface. She crossed the room and reached behind the swans to turn on the water faucets. The glazed, ceramic tiles winked at her from the shower walls as she adjusted the temperature. Then she noticed the gnarled, slimy hand curled around the edge of the curtain… waiting.

Margaret gasped. She tried to scream, but no sound came. Her mouth became a wordless oval which only surrendered a low disbelieving moan. Naked and defenseless, her body numbed. She staggered out of the bathroom clutching her throat and heaving for breath, only to back into a second being. The circle of her mouth grew larger and her eyes bulged as skeletal arms closed around her in a final embrace. The creature's chin came to rest on her shoulder. Though it possessed no vocal chords, the boney head seemed to breathe, "Mother's waiting," as it forced her toward the tub. The spindly, drippy arm from behind the curtain reached out to assist in the unholy baptism.

***

"She was never the same after her mother's death, poor dear," the cleaning woman informed the constable.

"How long ago did her mother pass?"

"Oh, heavens, years ago. And shortly after, Margaret became disabled. A fall in the bathtub. It was a freakish thing. Some say she tried to drown herself. Can you imagine? But she was always the skittish type. Seemed content to remain inside this house and let others handle what affairs needed tending."

"She was a recluse? Never went out?"

"Gracious, no. She's been bedridden for years. I come in to change the bed linens once a week,

when the nurse is off, you see. That's the best
I can do, coming all the way from town. I found
her like this." The neighbor quickly glanced at
Margaret, then turned away.

"An exam will determine the cause, but it's
natural, no doubt. Heart attack or stroke—one of
the usual suspects," the constable sighed.

"But what could have caused the horrible
expression on her face?" the woman asked, "As if
she died in absolute terror."

Margaret's eyelids were drawn up like tiny
silk curtains over her cataract-coated blue eyes
that appeared to see through the walls to a place
beyond. The constable mercifully lowered them.
"Who can say what one imagines in the final moment,
with the last gasp of life?" He pulled the sheet
over her face and waved the first response team
into the bedroom to remove the body of the old
woman who had lived alone for so long.

About the author:

Mr. Seate has written everything from humor to
the macabre. His short stories appear in several
magazines, anthologies and webzines. His two one-
author anthologies, Descent into Darkness and
From the Depths of Darkness, and his two suspense
thrillers, Chosen, and its sequel, Shanghai is
Crying are available through amazon.com and most
bookstores. Troy lives in Golden, Colorado.
Visit him on his website at www.geocities.com/
jtroyseate.

Bradd Parton

The One That Didn't Get Away

"These fish are about tired of you, Leon. You ain't caught a thing all day."

Kevin's voice sounded out of place along the serene bank of the creek, grating against the peaceful freshwater flow. He looked over at his friend, but Leon just sat there quietly, holding his fishing pole.

The two hadn't spoke in the hour since their argument. Kevin hoped giving him a hard time would make Leon snap out of it. He just wanted Leon to talk to him again, if only another of his vulgar insults.

"So where's that mouth of yours, now? Ain't you got somethin' smartass to say?"

Kevin's bravado never sounded convincing to Leon. There was no way he was going to fall for it.

Leon didn't budge.

"Whatever." Kevin's voice was meek as ever.

He wound his reel, bringing the line back. The bait was still there, untouched.

"Will you look at that? Not even a nibble. You might want to check your line, too."

Leon continued ignoring him.

"Fine, keep it up. Just remember who drove us here. You might end up walkin' back if you're gonna be a prick about it. I said I was sorry on account of the worms. You didn't have to cuss at me. I just forgot 'em."

For a moment, Kevin thought Leon was about to answer, but no—he just continued to sit there, not saying a word.

Kevin's fingers grew sticky as he pulled the soggy clump of bait from his hook and tossed it in the water. He reached over for a new piece, something fresh. Then, with a quick flick of his wrist, the line was back in the creek. The red and white float plopped under the surface of the water only to bounce back to the top, settling.

Kevin always hated it when he and his friend fought, but he never apologized unless he was truly at fault. And that just wasn't the case this time. It was Leon that started the fight, telling Kevin how stupid he was for forgetting the worms—again. Besides, at least he didn't cuss at Leon. Back when they were still on speaking terms, Leon let loose with all the four-letter words Kevin knew, and several he hadn't heard before, but certainly planned on using when the time presented itself.

Why *should* Kevin apologize? He couldn't *make* the fish bite. Minutes that seemed like hours passed.

Kevin finally relented. "Maybe they just ain't bitin' today, you know?"

He waited for his friend to say something like, "Probably because fish eat worms, stupid, not just any old thing."

But there was no reply from Leon.

The rhythmic crank of Kevin's reel went faster and faster as he drew in his line. "I think we might should give up on this creek, Leon. They just ain't hittin' on much…maybe I was wrong."

Out of the corner of his eye, Kevin watched Leon. For a moment, he thought he saw him smile. Maybe his friend was coming around, back to his old self.

But, no, Leon didn't speak, much less say he was sorry for yelling at Kevin.

"I know what, Leon! Maybe it's time we find some new bait. I bet that's just what we need, huh?"

Reaching over, Kevin wiggled the filet knife out of Leon's stiff neck with a wet pop. A buzz of disapproval sounded from the scattering flies. Leon's throat stood open, a smiling red gash. His arms and cheeks were smeared with blood, small chunks of flesh missing.

Three fingers were gone.

Both ears.

Kevin's handkerchief went red as he wiped the blood from the blade. He sucked a stray drop of it from his thumb.

His nose and eyes crinkled as he spoke. "I see why these fish ain't bitin', you tastin' like that."

"Well," Kevin said as he pulled up his own shirt, grabbing the chalky flab of his stomach. He flinched as the cold steel of the knife touched his pale skin, "I guess it's time to give 'em the good stuff."

About the author:

In addition to self-publishing his own comic series online and in print—3 issues to date—Bradd Parton's prose work was recently accepted for publication in an upcoming anthology edited by Scott Nicholson entitled *Little Shivers*

Jim Ehmann

Just Comes Natural

Joshua lay perfectly still, flat on his belly, on the sandy, rocky soil. Bracing his arms against the low boulder, he looked down the rifle sights at his next victim. He waited for the head to turn in his direction.

"All right, Uncle Lenny…it's your turn," he said, and then pulled the trigger.

With a pathetic, spastic leap, one more body hit the dirt and joined the other corpses littering the windy Colorado plain. Joshua reached inside his leather pouch for more bullets, but found none. "Dammit," he muttered.

Killing is about as fun as it gets, and Joshua wanted more.

Standing up and shaking the dust off his clothes, he pondered what to do with the bodies. They might be dead, but they still could be some fun. Joshua gathered his gear and walked down to the scene of the slaughter.

"One, two, three, four…" Joshua tallied the body count. Thirteen in all. A good number, he thought—one for each of his twelve years of age, and one to grow on, as his Pa would say.

He retrieved each dead prairie dog and carefully lined them up side by side in one neat, long row. Joshua giggled at the sight. The stupid critters looked like they were at the starting line, ready to run a race. "Who's gonna win? How 'bout you?"

he chuckled, picking one up by the stubby tail
and flinging it ahead.

Next Joshua assumed the persona of Preacher
Cooper from the church back in town and started
delivering eulogies for each prairie dog in
turn. After a few minutes he had an even better
idea. He fetched the prairie dog he had tossed
and propped the bloody little body up on its
hind legs, front paws draped over a small rock,
facing the others, ready to address the assembly
of executed rodents. Now, with Joshua's voice,
Preacher Dead Dog berated the rest for being
such worthless, filthy, no-good varmints. "You
all deserved to die, so burn in hell forever and
ever," he concluded.

Joshua could not bring himself to abandon his
harvest just yet. Pulling some rope from his
pack, he tied it snugly around the middle of each
prairie dog in sequence until they were laid out
like popcorn on a string. He shouldered his pack
and dragged the grisly bounty behind him as he
wandered back to the creek where he had left his
horse hitched to a cottonwood tree.

When he reached the old nag that his Pa had given
him, Joshua tied the rope off on the saddle and
started walking up the creek, leading the horse
by the reins. His triumphant hunt swelled Joshua
with ambition, and he worked his way upstream
further than ever before, into new territory.

Coming around a bend, Joshua discovered a
small, black hole a short distance up the hillside
on the other side of the creek. He figured it
was an old mine shaft; he had seen others when
out hunting with Pa. Pa always told him to
stay far away from them. But Pa was gone on a
cattle drive, and Joshua was stuck staying with
useless, drunk Uncle Lenny. Anything beat going

back to Lenny's pathetic shack, listening to the damn boozer singing his stupid songs. Other than drinking, singing, and sleeping, the only thing Lenny bothered with was finding some reason to give Joshua a whipping.

An attempt had been made to close off the mine shaft's entrance, but there was a hole bigger than a bucket between the broken timbers. In Joshua's imagination the jagged boards were monstrous fangs and the hole was the mouth of an incredible beast. He tied off the horse on a sapling and stared at the hole from the creek's edge. He grabbed a handful of rocks and took aim at the hole. On his third attempt, he hit the target and Joshua let out a whoop.

"Hey there, you," he called across to the monster. "You sure got a big, ugly mouth. You hungry? Look what I brought you." Joshua untied a pair of dead prairie dogs and took them down to the creek.

"Look here. Nice and fresh. Want one?" He picked up a dog by the tail and swung it back and forth a few times to test the weight. With an underhand sweep he let it fly with all his might towards the hole. Falling short, it rolled back down towards the creek. He had twelve more chances. Joshua focused hard and the fifth dog sailed across the creek and flew past the wooden teeth straight down the hole. He threw his arms up and gave a mighty holler.

He still had eight bodies left and it did not take Joshua long to come up with another plan. He scrounged the area and came up with a few short broken boards and some pieces of barbed wire. Binding the boards together with the wire, he fashioned a miniature raft. He removed three more prairie dogs from the rope and fit them onboard.

Joshua was crouching down at the water, preparing to launch the varmints on their journey downstream, when he heard a crackling, crunching sound. He looked up, across the creek. The sound came again—clearly from the hole. It reminded him of paper being crumpled, but it had a rhythmic, almost mechanical, character.

With a quick shove, the rodent raft slipped into the current. Joshua watched it for a few seconds as it floated away. Then he stood up, eyes fixed on the hole. He threw another rock, which struck just below the opening.

Almost immediately the sound came, louder, and something black flew out of the hole and landed on the hillside. Joshua stepped back, tripped, then got up and dashed over to his horse. Leaning up against the little tree, he stared back at whatever had come out of the hole.

Maybe a foot long, it had several long, black high-jointed legs that resembled a daddy-long-legs spider. The wings had made the crackling sound—like a giant grasshopper. They were folded up against the black body and hard to see. Joshua could not make out anything that looked like a head, although the body had a few short stalks protruding from it. The stalks seem to twist, probing the air.

The creature took a few slow, spidery steps down the hillside, then stopped. Joshua, frozen in fascination, held his breath. Suddenly, it leapt into the air with a flurry of metallic wings and landed at the base of the hill where Joshua's prairie dogs were piled up. The creature lifted its body high off the ground on its spindly legs and positioned itself over one of the bodies. Then it lowered onto the carcass and began to feed, using the mouth hidden on its underside.

After a few moments, the creature's body lifted up again. The insect-like wings unfolded and vibrated, making a high-pitched humming sound. The hum was answered by a commotion from the hole, and Joshua shrieked as several more creatures burst out of the hole. They quickly jumped or flew down and joined the first one at the feast.

Joshua watched in awe as the creatures stripped the dogs down to the bones in a matter of minutes. He could not see the teeth, but they sure did the job. Joshua was not easily scared—he had witnessed a stranger in town getting shot in the face, and had been right there when Leroy Simms was gored to death by a Texas Longhorn. Some overgrown bugs, or whatever, were not enough to make him run.

Soon the dozen or so creatures took a few steps off the carcasses, folded their legs up against their bloated bodies, and seemed to settle down. Two gave a brief hum with their wings before squatting down in the dirt.

Then all was quiet.

Joshua glanced over his shoulder at the sun, now getting low over the distant mountains. He needed to leave before long so he could get back before dark. If Uncle Lenny was still awake, he would get another whipping for being late for evening chores. But chances were good that his uncle was passed out in the hammock out back behind the shack. Lenny especially liked drinking on hot days like this.

Joshua kept watch for a bit longer then pulled out a little sack of grain for his horse. When the nag began munching on the oats, one of the creatures slowly rose up on its legs. It gave a short hop, then buzzed in to the air, crossing the creek and landing not twenty-five feet away from Joshua. The horse startled, and Joshua, nervous himself now, quickly untied the reins. He braced himself, but the creature just sat there, stalks twitching, but otherwise quiet.

One last bit of fun, thought Joshua. He untied one more prairie dog from the rope. Taking careful aim, he slung the body about ten feet to one side of the creature. Sure enough, the creature began creeping over to the offering. When it reached the body, the wings unfurled and it gave a long hum. Right away the other creatures across the creek began to stand up. One after another, they took to the air and crossed over, joining their leader.

Joshua had enough now. Shaking a little, he hurriedly mounted the horse and moved away to a more comfortable distance. Now a steady chorus of low hums filled the air.

"Ain't y'all had enough?" he called out bravely. "You sure are some hungry cusses."

Staying in the saddle, he reached down and hauled up the rope with the remaining prairie dogs. He removed two and awkwardly tossed them as far he could towards the creatures. Joshua quickly galloped off a good ways and then turned to watch. Like well trained pets, the creatures zoomed in and made short work of the dogs.

Whipping coming or not, it was time to get back to Uncle Lenny's place. The golden, sideways rays of the setting sun lit up Joshua's face; sitting straight up in the saddle, he shielded his eyes from the glare and looked back towards home. The day's events had left him feeling important, all grown up. Powerful, in a way. He turned to the humming, expectant creatures.

"You wanna go see if Uncle Lenny is sleeping?"

The creatures hummed their reply. Joshua spurred his horse into a trot. With short,

clattering flights, the black swarm followed
eagerly.

About the author:
Jim Ehmann is a Kentucky native living in
Portland, Oregon. He is a medical research grant
administrator. In addition to writing fiction,
he enjoys sixty-mile bike rides, Texas Hold'em
poker, Thai cooking, and the Portland Trailblazers
of the National Basketball Association. He
strongly prefers to write after midnight, much
to the dismay of his wife and two black cats.

Michelle Bredeson

Lone September Night

It was first the bloodcurdling scream that woke me from a deep sleep early the morning before my seventeenth birthday, then my best friend Janie kicking my legs in the bed next to me. My eyes struggled for sleep, refusing to acknowledge either disturbance. Janie and I and her twin brother, Wes, had stayed up much too late the night before telling ghost stories around their backyard fire pit. We would start our senior year of high school in just two days; my deeper concern, however, was the fact that I'd fallen in love with Wes over the course of the sweltering North Dakota summer.

"Haley, wake *up*!" Janie insisted as she used her foot to jab at my leg again. "Did you hear that?"

"What?" I moaned into my pillow.

"Duh—the *scream*."

"It's probably just Wes watching a movie or something," I assured her, refusing to open my eyes.

"He fell asleep on the couch before we came to bed, remember?"

"So? He probably woke up…"

Another scream, louder, closer, broke through the air. Janie clutched onto my arm, digging her nails into my skin. Now I was awake. I sat up and met her gaze in the dark room.

"What *was* that?" I whispered.

"I don't know," she whispered back.   She forced her fingernails further into my arm as she reminded me, "My parents are in Fargo for the weekend. It's just the three of us out here."

And no one else for miles.

My heart sped up. I had always loved the solitude of Janie's farmhouse, but not tonight. "It has to be Wes—playing a trick on us or something."

"I don't think so," she assured me.   "He wouldn't do anything to scare you."

"I wouldn't be so sure about that," I said as my eyes adjusted to the dark.   "Remember last year on my birthday when he put that wild raccoon in my car? It's definitely Wes."

"The screams didn't even sound like him," Janie said.   "Besides…"

"Besides what?" I asked as I forced myself from the bed. I grabbed a hoodie from the floor and slipped it on over my pajamas. "I'm going downstairs to scare the crap out of *him*. You want to come with me?"

A third scream found its way to my ears, shrill and high-pitched.   There was no way it had come from a man.

"That wasn't Wes," Janie confirmed as she jumped up from the bed.   "I told you he wouldn't scare you—not when he likes you so much."

My cheeks blazed as I turned to face her. "He what?"

"Nothing—I wasn't supposed to say anything," she said as she grabbed my arm again. "So, if it's not Wes, then who is it?"

I swallowed, looking to her bedroom door. "I don't know, I…Do you think Wes is okay? I mean, he was downstairs alone."

"I don't know, Haley. What should we do? My dad has a shotgun under his bed."

A loud *thud* sounded right outside the door. I let out the first shriek, and Janie mimicked my cry. We both jumped as the door flew open.

"Are you guys okay?" Wes asked as he flipped on the light.

I let out my breath as I looked him over. He bore his father's shotgun, and must have forgotten his shirt downstairs.

"If that was you, I'm going to *kill* you!" Janie exclaimed as she rushed up to slap his shoulder.

"That wasn't me," he said, his gaze flitting from his sister to me. "You alright, Haley?"

I shook my head as I crept up to Janie and took her hand in mine. "Is someone outside? Do you know who was screaming?"

"I thought maybe you two were playing a trick on me," he said, the corners of his mouth falling into a frown. "You know, payback for the raccoon, and the firecrackers in your locker that one time, and…"

"If it wasn't us, and it wasn't you, then someone has to be outside," Janie concluded.

"That's kind of what I was afraid of," Wes said, nodding toward the shotgun in his hand. "You two stay here—I'll go check it out."

"No!" I insisted, letting go of Janie to reach out for his arm. I quickly pulled my hand away when he met my eyes. "I mean, you can't go out there alone. What if someone's out there?"

"Haley, someone *is* out there," he said, his expression softening. "Besides, I'm a great shot with this thing. I'll be right back."

"No!" Janie protested this time. "That's what they always say in the movies right before they're killed by the escaped mental patient or vampire or whatever."

Wes rolled his eyes. "Tell you what—if I find Edward Cullen out there I'll make sure to get his autograph for you.　I'll be right back, I *promise*."

I found Janie's hand again and pulled her out into the hall right after her brother.

"So you're coming with me then?" he asked as he turned to meet my gaze.

I flashed a crooked smile.　"If Edward Cullen *is* out there, I don't want to miss it."

He let out a laugh, shaking his head as he reached the staircase.　"We're most likely to find Kyle out there.　Best friend, my ass.　He was supposed to go camping with his cousin tonight, but he might have made a detour to our place since he knows Mom and Dad are out of town."

"So you think *Kyle's* playing a joke on us?" Janie asked as we flooded onto the first floor.

"I think someone is," Wes assured her.　"We're in the middle of nowhere, Sis.　Nothing ever happens in the middle of nowhere."

I hoped he was right as we crept toward the front door.　I watched carefully as Wes reached out for the knob, and grabbed his hand before he had the chance to open it. He took in his breath as he turned to face me.

"Haley?" he whispered.

"Just…be careful," I instructed, and promptly released him.

He nodded, and opened the door. "Stay inside," he commanded as he stepped onto the large front porch.　I wanted to follow him anyway, but Janie kept me beside her just inside the doorframe.

Wes raised the shotgun to his shoulder as he made a semicircle to look around the yard.　He let out a sigh as he lowered the weapon a few moments later.　I hadn't seen anything either.

"Hello!" Wes called out, his voice echoing through the quiet night.　There was only dead silence in return. He waited a few moments and then said, "Kyle? Is that you…? Look, I told you Haley won't go out with you so if you're trying to get her attention…"

A scream erupted through the night again, and Wes had the gun back on his shoulder, cocked, in half a second. He cursed, his back rigid as he made another sweep of the yard. I peered out from behind him, but only noted the empty country road several hundred yards ahead, and the blackness of spruce trees surrounding the farmyard.

"I want you two back in the house, now," Wes insisted, his gaze darting around the dark night.

"No," Janie told him. "We're staying with you!"

"Damnit, Janie, just do what I tell you!" he snapped. "Go into Dad's office and get your and Mom's handguns from the safe. There should be loaded clips in there, too. I want you to each take one and meet me back here. Now, Janie!"

She nodded and dragged me back through the living room, dining room, and into her dad's office. I watched as her shaking hands found the combination on the gun safe lock. She pulled out the handguns and gave one to me. She handed me a full clip and I shoved it into the gun just as Wes and their dad had shown me time and again. I left the safety on as we traipsed back through the house to the front door.

Wes was still on the porch, gun at his shoulder, finger at the trigger, frozen.

"Keep the safeties on until I say," he ordered.

"Do you really think we'll need to use them?" Janie asked.

"I hope to hell not, but someone is out there and I'm pretty certain it's not Kyle. He wouldn't take too well to a loaded gun aimed his way."

"So what should we do?" I found myself asking.

"For now we wait," he assured me without looking back. "I think the screams are coming from the east, but I can't be sure. You okay with that gun in your hand, Haley?"

"S-sure," I squeaked.

"It'll be just like target practice," he assured me. "Remember all those Coke cans you made a mess of? Well, it'll be just like that."

There was another shriek, closer this time. Wes had been right; they were coming from the east. We all turned that way, straining to see through the dark.

"Maybe we should go out there?" Janie whispered. "The coyotes haven't been scared to come up to the house at night. What if someone was out for a walk? What if someone's hurt and they need our help?"

"No one we know would be walking ten miles out of town at three o'clock in the morning," Wes assured her. "Besides, anyone around here would know this is our farm—they'd be calling out Dad's name or something."

"What if it isn't someone from around here?" I questioned. "What if it's someone passing through?"

"On a country road in the middle of the night? I doubt it. Besides, a car hasn't gone by all night—I would have heard it."

"Okay, so if it's nothing obvious then what is it, Wes?" I insisted. "Because you're right—this is pretty much the gold standard for the middle of nowhere. Someone's out there and they're probably hurt. We shouldn't be pointing guns at them. I should call my dad."

"We don't need a doctor—not yet," Wes assured me.

"Well, we should call *someone*."

"Like who?" Janie asked. "The sheriff?"

"We're not calling Sheriff Johnson out here for no reason," Wes said.

"No reason?" I asked. "You're the one pointing a gun at absolutely nothing! I'm calling him."

"Wait!" Wes said, lowering the shotgun. "You're right, okay? But what if it's nothing?"

"It's *something*," Janie said. "Someone was screaming. We need to call someone. I'll call Dad."

"You're not calling Dad," Wes growled. "It's their nineteenth anniversary, Janie."

"Then we should call Haley's dad."

Wes looked to me and let out a deep sigh. "Do you really think we should call your dad?"

"Yes, I do. Look, you're quite capable of taking care of us, Wes, but someone could be hurt. My dad won't mind—it's his job to help people."

"Fine," he conceded. "Take my sister with you, and don't set down those guns."

"Yes, sir," I smirked, and grabbed Janie's arm to lead her into the kitchen. I flipped on the light, squinting for a moment as my eyes adjusted to the brightness. Janie set her gun on the counter to pull a can of Coke from the fridge. I kept my gun in my hand as I picked up the cordless phone.

"There's no dial tone," I said as I turned to Janie.

"No dial tone?" she asked as she popped the tab on her Coke. "Are you sure?"

"Yes, I'm sure. I know what no dial tone sounds like."

"Here, use this," she said as she picked up Wes's cell from the counter.

I frowned as I took it from her and flipped it open.   I punched in my home number and pressed send.

"Well?" Janie asked.

"It's not ringing."

"What do you mean, it's not ringing?"

I put the phone up to her ear.   "It's not ringing."

"Maybe you did it wrong," she said, and hung it up before she typed in the number again.

I rolled my eyes.   "I know how to use a cell phone, Janie."

"Yeah, but it's not yours so you never…It's not ringing."

"Yeah, like I said.   My cell's in my purse in the living room.   I'll go get it."

"Wait!" Janie hollered.

"What?" I demanded, my chest fluttering as I met her gaze.

"I'm coming with you.   Wes said to stick together, remember?"

"You didn't have to give me a heart attack in the process," I told her as we stepped into the living room.   I dug through my purse for my cell as Janie turned on a lamp.   "Of course."

"Of course what?"

"Dead battery—and I left my charger at home."

"Of course.   My cell's upstairs."

"What the hell's taking so long?" Wes called from the porch.

"Phones aren't working!" Janie called back.

"What?" he demanded as he stormed into the living room.   "What do you mean they're not working?"

"The landline's dead, and your phone's broken or something—it won't even ring."

"And mine has a dead battery," I said as I threw it on the coffee table.

"I used my phone just a few hours ago," Wes said, heading for the kitchen. Janie and I followed him and watched as he picked up the cell and brought it to his ear. He frowned as he turned to us again. "If this is a joke I'm going to kill you guys."

"Would you get over yourself! We're not trying to trick you," I informed him. "Our phones are dead and someone or something's outside."

"Are all the phones dead?" Wes asked, looking to me.

"We haven't tried Janie's—it's upstairs."

He nodded, still clutching onto the shotgun as he rushed out of the room.

"This is way too weird," Janie noted as she set her soda on the counter. "If the phones aren't working, I say we leave. We'll take my dad's truck and head into town. The sheriff can come back here and figure out what the heck's going on."

"Your phone is dead, too!" Wes called from upstairs. He returned wearing a sweatshirt, the shotgun still in his left hand. "Screw this—we're taking Dad's truck and heading into town. We'll call the sheriff from your house, Haley."

"Sure," I said as he headed for the garage door. The lights went out just as he reached for its handle.

Janie yelped, clawing for my arm.

"Hey, it's okay," Wes said. "The power going out doesn't mean anything. Let's just get in the truck. I think there's a flashlight around here somewhere." On his last word a thin beam of light filled the room. He flashed it in his sister's face and she drew up her hand to shield her eyes. "You're going to be okay. I'm not going to let anything happen to you." He caught

my gaze and added, "Either of you." He opened
the door to the garage, walked inside. "Watch
your step. Can you see to get into the truck?"

"Yeah, I think so," I told him as he opened
the passenger door. "Shouldn't the interior
light have come on?"

"Yes," he sighed as he climbed inside the cab.
I craned my neck and watched as he slid the key
into the ignition. "Shit."

"It's not starting?" Janie asked.

"It's not doing anything," he confirmed.

"Is the battery dead?" I asked.

"Maybe. Let's try my car and see what happens."
I jumped when he reached out and took my hand
in his. "Sorry—just thought this would be best
if we're heading outside. I don't want to lose
track of either of you."

"Sure," I said, squeezing his fingers as I
laced my free arm through Janie's. I took in my
breath as we spilled out the door, and walked
as close to Wes as I dared without tangling my
feet in his. "It sure is dark without the yard
light."

"You've got that right," he said as we reached
the Ford Contour he shared with Janie. He turned
off the flashlight as he slid into the driver's
seat, put the key in the ignition.

"Well?" I whispered, my eyes glancing around
the dark yard. The sliver of moon and clouded
sky offered little insight as to what may be
looming in the trees. "Wes?"

He let out a string of curses. "I wish I knew
what the hell was going on."

"It's not starting?" Janie asked as she wrapped
both arms around my waist.

Wes climbed out of the car and slammed the
door shut. "Shit!"

"Hey," I said as I took his hand in mine again. He seemed to calm as I ran my thumb across his fingers. "We're going to be okay. We could take a tractor, or the four-wheeler even. And doesn't your dad have a CB radio in the shop?"

He let out a deep sigh. "Yeah, he does. I'll go check it out."

"Yeah, right," I said as I squeezed my fingers around his. "We're coming with you, Wes."

"You still have that gun?"

"I do. Janie left hers in the kitchen."

"Well, two will have to do." He turned on the flashlight and waved it across the farmyard as we walked to the shop. There was no movement, no sound. As far as I could tell we were as good as alone.

The shop door creaked as Wes swung it open. Janie jumped, both of her arms still around my waist. I clung to Wes as we stepped inside the shop, his flashlight barely showing a free path.

"Where's the CB?" I questioned, making sure I kept my voice cool.

"In the back corner here," Wes said as we crept along. "You guys okay?"

"I guess," Janie squeaked. "The CB should work, right? I mean, if anything should work, the CB should work."

"Hope so," Wes sighed as we reached a long oak table. He let go of my hand and gave me the flashlight, then propped his gun against the wall beside him. I searched his gaze as I held the light over the table. He was trying not to show it, but I knew he was just as terrified as I was.

"Well?" Janie asked as Wes fiddled with the CB.

"Give me a second, okay?"

"Hey, Janie," I said as I wrapped my arm around her shoulders. "Did you tell Wes about your date with Seth last Friday night?"

"You went out with Seth Jackson?" Wes snickered.

I grinned, thankful I had managed to lighten the mood.

"It was just one date," Janie assured him.

"Liar," I quipped.

"You do realize he's going off to college tomorrow," Wes noted. "You're not going to see him again until Thanksgiving, if that."

"Nice—relationship advice from the master," she said as he kept working on the radio. "When was the last time you had a date exactly? Oh that's right—prom."

"It's not for lack of options," he assured her. His fingers moved over the same buttons again and again, but the damned thing just would not come to life. He looked up to Janie, then to me. "Nothing. I'm sorry—I don't know what else to do."

"We haven't heard anything in what, at least five minutes?" Janie questioned. "Maybe whoever's out there is okay now. Maybe they don't need us."

We jumped in unison as a scream rattled through the air. Wes picked up the shotgun in one swift movement, and I soon found my arm around his waist. Janie was clutching onto us both; we were all so close that I could hear their hearts pounding.

"Okay, we need to calm down," Wes decided.

"I think we should go back into the house," I told him. "At least we have cover there."

"Sure, good plan," he said. "Janie, you're going to have to give me some room in case I need to use this gun."

"Haley won't let go of you either," she said.

"Wes is right," I said as I pulled away from him. "Wes, you should go out first, then Janie, then me. We'll grab the other gun again once we're back inside."

"I can't believe you left your gun," Wes mumbled as he started toward the door.

My heart raced as I followed after them. We should have stayed in the house, even if the power was out. Anything would have been better than having to face the night again.

"The good news is it will be dawn in just a couple hours," Wes said as he reached the door. He took in a deep breath before walking back into the vacant night. I had to force oxygen into my lungs as I followed after his lead. "And then it's just one more day until your birthday, Haley."

"Yeah, my birthday," I said, my gaze flitting every which way as we walked through the brisk air. There was nothing but the black void of trees and absolute haunting silence.

"Are we all still going to the movies?" Wes questioned. "I mean, is that still the plan?"

"Mm-hmm," I mumbled.

"You don't, like, have a date or something instead, do you, Haley?"

"Oh, I," I said, my gaze landing on him for a moment before I turned back to the trees. "No, just you. I mean, I'm just hanging out with Janie and you."

"We should go to your house after," Wes said, his posture stiff, his finger ever at the trigger. "We could play Monopoly, or I could beat you at Tetris again."

"You've never beat me at Tetris," I reminded him as we reached the door.

He turned and grinned, and I realized he had been doing his best to keep me calm until we reached the house again. He tried to turn the knob.

"It's locked." He pulled a set of keys from his pocket, shoved one into the lock. He twisted it until his knuckles were white. "Shit, I can't get it open."

"What do you mean, *you can't get it open*?" Janie insisted. She stepped in front of her brother and twisted the handle again and again, but it would not budge. "We never lock the house, Wes. We don't need to lock it because we live in North Dakota and nothing ever happens here!"

I wrapped my free arm around her shoulders, and clicked the safety off my gun. "Janie, it's going to be okay. Wes said he's not going to let anything happen to us and he's not." I locked eyes with him and he nodded. "This isn't the only door—we'll try another and we'll be inside in no time."

"Let's try the back door," Wes said. "Take the safety off that gun, Haley."

"I'm one step ahead of you."

"Of course you are," he said, and caught my gaze before he headed for the back door.

I struggled to keep Janie on her feet while scanning the yard. I did not see anything; not one single solitary movement. I clenched my teeth together, waiting for the next scream. It was just a matter of time before it happened again.

Wes tried the door, but I figured it was locked before he had a chance to say so. Even so, he struggled with it until the key broke off in the lock. Janie started crying—small whimpers at first, but they soon turned into dramatic sobs. I frowned as I met Wes's gaze again. He held my eyes, shaking his head slightly.

"Well," I whispered, glancing at Janie. She was trembling now, and I was supporting most of her weight. "Where else can we go?"

Wes swallowed, staring over my face. "The doors won't open."

"I know."

"The phones aren't working."

"I know."

"The cars won't start."

"Wes, I know," I said as I moved my hand from Janie to rest it on his arm. "But I need you right now, okay? You can't fall apart on me, too. Where else can we go?"

He sucked in his breath as I clutched onto Janie again. "I don't know if it'd be safe."

I let out a small laugh. "Like we're safe right now?"

He nodded. "There's a small loft in the shop. If we go up there we'd be trapped, but at least we'd know if someone was coming after us."

"Then we'll go there. Do you have any more ammunition?"

"My dad has some stashed in the shop."

"Is there anything else in there? Blankets or anything? Wesley!"

"Yes, I'm sorry—yes."

"Show me," I insisted.

"Do you really think that's our best option?"

"I think it's our *only* option," I assured him. "You're right—the sun will be up in just a couple hours. We can hold out until then."

"We don't even know what's happening, Haley."

I looked once again to Janie, who was still sobbing into my shoulder. "Yes, but we can't keep running around all night like this. We have to get somewhere safe and we have to calm her down."

He wiped his brow with the back of his hand. "You're right. Let's try the shop again. Maybe we'll have better luck there."

"Let's go," I said, and led the way. Adrenaline replaced horror with each step.   I knew that even if Janie and Wes were not strong enough to make it through the night, I had to be. Wes was right, none of us knew what was happening, but we could still find a way to survive it.

"Wes, the flashlight," I said as I reached the door to the shop.   It was still open, and hopefully as quiet as we had left it.

He stepped in front of me, and scanned the light over the small space.   I noted the riding lawn mower this time, and the '72 Mustang that Wes's dad had been restoring for the past three years. Nothing seemed out of place, but I knew that did not mean anything.

"Come on," Wes said as he rushed across the room to a large tool chest. He pulled out two boxes of shotgun shells before stepping over to a ladder. "I'll go up first."

"No, I should go," I told him.

"No way! What if someone's up there?"

"If it came down to it, you'd do a much better job of taking care of your sister than I would," I said. Janie was still crying as I let go of her to grab onto the ladder. I debated whether or not to leave off the safety of my gun, and decided it would be better if I did not accidentally shoot myself. I clicked the safety on and reached for the ladder again.

"Wait!" Wes cried in a hushed whisper.

"What?" I asked as I turned to meet his gaze.

"Take the flashlight," he said as he handed it to me.

"Then you take my gun," I said as I set it in his palm. I secured the flashlight in my left hand before I grabbed onto the ladder once more.

"Wait!" Wes called out again.

"What?" I snapped.

"Haley, I…"

"What, Wes? I'm kind of in the middle of something here."

"I want to take you to the movies on your birthday."

"We're already going to the movies on my birthday," I reminded him as I began to climb the ladder.

"No, I know. I mean, I want to take you to the movies just the two of us."

I paused, my heart now racing, for a much different reason. "Like just me and you and not your sister?"

"Yeah."

"Okay," I said, and continued up the ladder. I hesitated as I reached the top, sure I was going to find some kind of monster waiting to ambush me. I summoned all the courage I had and raised the flashlight to scan the small loft. It was empty. "Janie, come up!" I told her as I crawled onto the wooden floor. I peered over the edge and stared down at my best friend. "It's safe—promise."

"Take this," Wes said as he shoved the handgun at her. "And be careful."

She nodded, and started up the ladder.

I shone the flashlight down on her, but my gaze soon fixed on Wes. He had walked away from the ladder, and I could not make out what he was doing. "Wes, where the hell are you going?"

"Blankets, remember?" he said, stepping back to the ladder just as Janie reached the top.

I grabbed onto her arms and hoisted her up next to me. She fell into a heap, and clutched onto my arm as a new flood of tears made their way to her eyes. I ignored her as I peered down from the loft, giving Wes as much light as I could.

My stomach was in knots as I watched him struggle to get up the ladder with an armful of blankets and that loaded shotgun. I knew I would not be anything close to calm until he was next to me again. "You doing okay?"

"I'm fine," he muttered.

"This was a really great idea, Wes. You always were too smart for your own good."

"You're just saying that so I won't drop anything."

Another bloodcurdling scream rang through the air, echoing off the thin shop walls. Wes lost his grip on the ladder and fell to the floor in a loud *thud*. He scrambled to his feet and started up the ladder again.

"Wes, if you're not up here in five seconds I'm going to kick your ass!" I growled, my gaze intent on him. I grabbed the gun from his hands as soon as I could reach it, then the blankets. I set them down next to Janie as Wes climbed into the loft with us.

I threw my arms around his neck before he had his balance, and held him in a tight hug. His arms tightened around me as he buried his face in my hair. "Are you okay?" I asked, refusing to let go of him just yet.

"Yeah, I'm okay."

I squeezed onto him for a few moments more before pulling away. "Did it sound closer this time?"

"Yeah," Wes said, catching my gaze as I turned to Janie. I shook out one of the blankets before I wrapped it around her shoulders. She curled into a ball on the floor, tears streaking down her cheeks as she closed her eyes tight. I rested my hand on her shoulder before I met Wes's gaze again. He was frowning, and there was alarm in his eyes. "Did it sound closer to you, too?"

I nodded as he picked up the flashlight. He leaned over the ladder and swept the soft beam across the shop floor. "Nothing."

"Good."

"Honestly the screams aren't what's freaking me out. The house being locked…"

"I know, Wes."

He took in his breath as he sat up next to me. "And the phones and the cars…"

"The important thing is we're all okay."

"I know, but…what is it, Haley? I mean, seriously, what could it be?"

I reached out for his hand and held it in mine. "I don't know."

He caught my eyes and said, "Something's out there."

"You're right, but I don't know what we should do about it."

Wes let go of my hand and reached across me to grab the shotgun again. He checked to make sure the safety was on before he set it down next to him. He settled in right beside me, so close that his shoulder was touching mine.

"Janie?" Wes asked, looking to his sister. "You okay?"

She whimpered, but did not give any further response.

I ran my hand along her shoulder before resting it on top of her arm. "We're going to be alright, Janie. You're brother's taking good care of us."

Wes smirked, and I turned to face him again. "Haley, I'm not…"

"You're not what?" I whispered.

"We're stuck in the shop loft in the middle of the night. Janie's obviously freaking out. I have absolutely no idea what to do next. I mean, I should have handled this better."

"Handled it better how?" I asked. "Wes, you've done everything right."

"We shouldn't have left the house."

"We didn't know what would happen if we did."

He shook his head. "I'm sorry I let you down."

"You didn't let anyone down, Wes. Should we turn off the flashlight? We should save the battery."

He nodded. "Janie, is it okay if I turn off the flashlight?"

She let out a low grumble, which I took for a yes. Wes must have too because he distinguished the light. I blinked a few times as my eyes adjusted to the dark. It was pitch black at first, but soon faded into a blotchy dismal coal.

"Can you see anything?" Wes whispered as he inched closer to me.

"Not really. Can you?"

"No," he said as he brushed his fingertips over the top of my hand. "I don't hear anything, though. Do you?"

"No, I don't hear anything."

"If the screams are so far away, what do you think happened to the phones and the cars? Who do you think locked the doors to the house?"

A shiver raced up my spine as I speculated answers. "Maybe it's better we don't know."

"Maybe," he said as he wrapped his fingers around mine.

I moved my hand until it was tight in his. "Wes, I'm scared."

"Yeah, me too."

I rested my head on his shoulder, my eyes still scanning the dark shop. Just because it was silent did not mean we were alone. "So are you ready to go back to school?"

He let out a small laugh. "Am I ready to go back to school? Yeah, I don't know. I made a lot of money working construction this summer. I'd honestly rather do that."

"I guess," I sighed.

"Do you know what you're getting for your birthday?"

"No, what'd you get me?"

He squeezed my hand, and I noted a smile on his face. "That's a surprise, Haley. You'll just have to wait."

I managed a grin as I looked back to the shop floor. There was still no movement, no sound. Whoever had been screwing with us before seemed content to leave us alone, at least for now.

"My dad's putting a new stereo in my car," I informed him. "And I'm sure my mom has something planned, too. Being an only child has its benefits."

"I guess it would. I sure like my sister, though. I wouldn't trade her for anything in the world."

"Don't blame you there," I noted as I traced my fingers along Janie's arm. "I think she might be asleep."

"Thank God for small favors. I'm honestly surprised you're holding it together so well."

"You're not the only one. I guess I just had to make sure Janie was okay. I had to make sure you were okay, too."

"Well, for now I'm okay, but the sun hasn't come up yet."

"I think whoever's out there isn't hurt," I concluded. "The screams would have been more consistent, don't you think? They're too far apart, too sporadic."

"Yeah, I think you're right. So what do you think it is then? I mean, who would do this?"

"No one we know. No one from town."

"I still can't figure out why the house is locked. I mean, the cars and the phones…that's weird, yes, but the house…the house just baffles me."

"Then let's not think about it," I said. "Let's think about anything except that. Janie's asleep. If she was able to stop thinking about it, then we can, too."

"Okay, here's a question. Why didn't you tell me she's dating Seth?"

"Because I didn't know it was my responsibility to keep you updated on her love life."

"It's not, I guess, but you're my friend, too. It wouldn't hurt to keep me informed about what's going on with you two."

"I'll try to remember that."

"Like did you date anyone this summer?"

"What?" I demanded, heat filling my cheeks.

"You and Grady hung out a few times."

"You think I'd go out with Grady? I guess you don't know me as well as you thought."

"So you don't have a boyfriend or anything then?"

"No," I said, meeting his gaze. "I don't have a boyfriend. I'm sure you'd know if I did. News travels pretty fast around here."

"I suppose it does."

"So what should we do when the sun comes up?" I asked. "Or have you thought about that?"

"Yeah, I've thought about it. We're going to walk to the Henderson farm and hope to God their phones are working. It's three miles away, but we should be okay to walk that far in the light."

"What time do you think it is?"

"Four, maybe?"

"This is the longest night of my life."

"I know what you mean."

"Do you think the sheriff will find anything when he comes tomorrow?" I questioned.

Wes squeezed my hand for a moment. "God, I hope so."

"No offense, but I wish Janie would have stayed at my house tonight."

Wes laughed. "Yeah, I kind of wish I'd stayed there, too."

"After tonight you might want to."

"No shit."

"So what movie do you want to see?" I asked, meeting his eyes through the dark.

"It's your birthday—shouldn't you pick?"

"Yeah, but Janie and I were going to go see a chick flick. I don't want to subject you to that."

"Why not? Like I said, it's your birthday."

"So you'll go see whatever I pick? No matter what it is?"

"Yep."

I rolled my eyes. "You must really like me then."

"Yep."

It hit me what I said, what *he* said, and my gaze fell back to the shop floor. It was still quiet, and for some reason that scared me. I could not help but to wonder what was going on outside in the farmyard and the woods beyond that we were not seeing.

"Haley?"

"Yeah?"

"You okay? I mean, you're quiet."

"There's just a lot to think about tonight."

"I guess there is. Look, about your birthday."

"What about it?" I asked, looking to him again.

"If you don't want to do something with me—I mean with *just* me—I understand."

I looked over his face that I had come to think was so beautiful in the past few months. He was not just my best friend's brother, he was my other best friend. He was the person I wanted to go to every movie with, no matter what it was, just the two of us.

"Haley?"

I took in a deep breath as I decided to kiss him. What did I have to lose at this point? I let out my breath, and brought my lips to his.

Wes kissed me back and I pulled away.

"I'm…are you alright?" he asked.

"Yes."

"Okay."

We sat in silence for a moment. I was not quite sure what to do next. This was what I wanted, but I was also overwhelmed with how this would change everything between us. What would Janie think?

"Haley, look I…" Wes started as another random scream flooded the air.

I threw my arms around his waist as he reached for the shotgun again. I looked to Janie, but she was fast asleep. I hoped we would not need a reason to disturb her.

"I'm scared," I admitted in a hushed whisper.

"I think that's all this is—someone trying to scare us."

"It's working."

Wes sighed as he wrapped his arm around my shoulders. "The sun should be up soon. We're almost through the night."

"Can we keep talking? About anything? I'll feel better if we keep talking."

"Sure," Wes said, and indulged me with his plans for the basketball team the coming year and how he thought he would work construction again

next summer.   I held onto him as I listened,
waiting for the next scream to fill the air.

***

The night was good to us after that, and the
sun came up without any further disturbances.
Wes waited until we had a good hour of daylight
before he woke Janie.   He crept down from the
loft first, shotgun in hand, and made sure all was
clear before he let either me or his sister join
him on the shop floor.

The sun blazed in the sky as we followed Wes
outside.   He headed for the Contour first, and
tried the key once more.   The engine turned over
right away, and I frowned as Wes found my eyes.

Whatever had troubled us in the night seemed
long gone.

We piled into the car and Wes sped away from
the farm without a word.   He drove straight to
the Sheriff's station; though our stories seemed
farfetched an investigation was launched.   Even
after a thorough search through the woods around
the farmstead, nothing was ever found.

Janie did not sleep at her house again for
over a month, and it took Wes almost as long.   He
still sleeps with a loaded shotgun under the bed,
and every night I consider doing the same.   I ask
him every so often what he thinks that night was,
what really went on out there, but he never has
an answer for me.

I still do not have any answers, either, but I
am certain of one thing—I would give up everything
I have for just one glimpse of the faceless
monsters that haunted us that lone September
night.

About the author:

Michelle Bredeson grew up in a small town in South Dakota and frequented her grandparents' farm often as a child. At eighteen she moved to North Dakota and spent most of her adult life there. Although she has lived in the Twin Cities the past two years, she will contend that the scariest place imaginable is a lone country road, in the middle of the night, surrounded by dark, with only a sliver of moon to light her path. Follow her blog at evidentlyandofcourse. blogspot.com/.

Jack Burton

The Cabin

"I wonder if this little guy has been impregnated by a wasp?" Jeff asked, bringing a small stick towards the caterpillar who, in turn, rose up in an attack stance.

"What?" Morgan queried, hoping she had misheard her husband, but knowing deep down she had not.

"The Glyptapanteles wasp," Jeff answered, dropping the twig and turning to his wife. "They use mind control on caterpillars, you know."

Morgan sighed quietly and walked up to the caterpillar's tree branch, pretending to care.

"That particular wasp will inject eggs inside a caterpillar. But unlike other wasps, the Glyptapanteles actually turns the caterpillar into its slave, or living zombie, so to speak." Jeff grinned. He was so excited about sharing the knowledge that he barely picked up on the fact that Morgan was not quite as thrilled. "After impregnation, the caterpillar goes on with its life while the baby wasps feed off its innards. The wasps eventually drill their way out of the caterpillar and spin cocoons on the branches next to him. They will grow into adults inside the cocoon."

"Sounds fascinating," Morgan commented.

"That's not even the coolest part," Jeff continued, mistaking her comment for genuine enthusiasm. "The caterpillar doesn't die after the wasps come out. Instead it sits on the branch and guards the cocoons. The caterpillar won't

eat or roam away. It disregards its own needs
to protect the wasp cocoons. If a predator comes
close, the caterpillar will attack the intruder.
When the adult wasps finally emerge from the
cocoon, the caterpillar's job is complete—and it
dies!"

"That's pretty crazy," Morgan replied after
the in-depth explanation.

"I know! Somehow the wasps force the
caterpillar to be their bodyguard. Like I said,
a zombie slave!" Morgan attempted to speak but
Jeff continued, "I don't see any cocoons here,
but this sort of mind control *actually happens*
in parasites throughout the wild. Venom or
secretions chemically change the host's behavior,
but I don't think scientists will ever have it
completely figured out."

Morgan knew that the information would have
interested her if the past year and a half had
not been filled with similar and equally useless
information on arachnids, insects and other random
animals. Morgan knew about Jeff's fascination
with nature when they got married. He *was* a
professor of Biology at the Community College
in Beaver County, and she supported his love
for his work, but there was a time and place for
everything. Lately, Jeff was unable to find that
balance.

He was more passionate about his job and study
of the bug world than he was in their marriage.

"It is interesting honey, but this weekend I
just want to enjoy nature—not learn about it.
That's why we came to the cabin."

And to save our marriage.

"Sorry." His smile dropped. "I thought you
enjoyed this."

"I do!" She took his hand in hers. "I do,
but sometimes it's too much. I want to sit with

you on the rocks and watch the brook trickle by without learning how algae supports all aquatic life."

He nodded.

"Or hold hands and gaze up at the night sky without an astronomy lesson. It takes away some of the magic and wonder." She smiled, hoping he would understand and realize that she loved him dearly. She needed *him* for the weekend—not Professor Dillon, just Jeff, her husband.

"I understand. I do get carried away sometimes." He pulled her into his chest and wrapped his arms around her. "Let's get to the creek and afterwards we can sit by the fire or under the stars. Your choice."

When they arrived at the water's edge, they found giant boulders, and remained there for some time, skipping stones and just relaxing. On a few occasions Jeff caught himself about to rattle off some interesting facts about the Black Moshannon Bog, which was also located in the Pennsylvania Wilds, but quickly let the thoughts go. By the time they returned to the cabin, Morgan was pleased to have the Jeff she married back.

"How about I light that fire, throw down a blanket and bring out two glasses of champagne?"

"Oh Jeffrey," Morgan swooned in an exaggerated manner. "You know just how to treat a lady." She caught sight of the hatchet hanging by the fireplace. "Is my big, burly woodsman gonna chop some wood for us?" They laughed as Jeff puffed out his chest trying to act the role. Jeff was built like the stereotypical college professor—he might have been able to tip the scales at one sixty-five, but that was only if he was soaking wet, with clothes on.

"Actually we have a few logs in there already, and I think that will last us the night. Besides, it's getting dark, and with my outdoor skills I'll end up missing the wood completely and burying the blade in my leg."

"Ah, so romantic," she teased.

"I try."

"Here's the plan. You set everything up while I take a shower," she smiled.

This was the Jeff she loved.

"It's a deal." They kissed and Morgan sauntered away to the bath inside the master bedroom.

Jeff smiled and watched her athletic hips sway from side to side as she departed. There was something special about being up north again, in the cool, fresh air, and the cabin which had become a meaningful hideout from civilization for the both of them.

Despite being a state park, most of the land was privately owned, and there were rarely any hikers or tourists to bother them. A small number of paths ran from the main road, but they were unpaved. Their closest neighbors, in the rural Pennsylvania forest, were miles away.

The isolation was never a problem for the couple. If anything, it added extra spice and excitement to the magic moments they had created over the years. Jeff had proposed in front of the very fireplace he now readied. Five years ago, he had used the same one-kneed stance to start their life together.

He lit the kindling and watched the smoke rise past the discolored bricks. The sight and smell of the flames allowed all the happy memories to flood through him, and in their wake, the tension of the past year washed away.

With the flames rising, Jeff laid out a puffy quilt and several pillows. He popped a chilled bottle of Perrier Jouët and filled two flutes. Quite pleased with himself, he surveyed the romantic setting.

A piercing scream rang through the cabin, shattering his thoughts.

He rushed to the bathroom and saw Morgan flat on her back on the floor, her legs splayed on the rim of the tub. The glass shower door was broken, and Morgan was flailing her arms violently about her face.

"Get it off of me!" she shouted in terror.

"Morgan!" he knelt next to her, trying to grab hold of her arms. "It's me."

She struck him twice before realizing it was her husband and she was safe. He nestled her head in his arms and she started to bawl.

"Baby, it's okay. I'm here. You're all right."

"It got me," she looked up at him with wide eyes. "It got me!"

"Nothing's got you babe," Jeff reassured her.

"Look," she said, wiping translucent goo from the side of her mouth.

"It's just spit," Jeff said and raised her off the floor, careful not to cut her on the shards of glass.

"It attacked me!" She pressed her shivering, wet body against his.

"Let me see your back," he said, examining the small wounds. The glass had left only minor scratches. "Thank God you're okay. That glass could have sliced you to ribbons if you fell on it the wrong way."

"Jeff," she pulled away and looked into his eyes, "You're not listening to me! I was attacked!" Her body still heaved with adrenaline.

"Honey, no one is here. You're just in shock."

"It wasn't a person," she said slower, trying to regain her composure. "It was some kind of

animal! It jumped at my face and I tried to
scream, but my mouth…" She took several deeps
breaths, knowing that if she finished her thought,
she would start to hyperventilate.

"Your mouth…?" Jeff asked confused.

"I don't know," she finished. "It was on me
for what felt like an eternity, but I suppose it
was only a few seconds. I blacked out when I
fell through the door, but came to right away.
This *thing* was on me and I felt wetness—I was
gagging on it. I managed to hit it away and
finally scream."

"Probably just a large tarantula," Jeff said,
wrapping a robe around her naked body. "We need
to spray the place again. That's all."

She shook her head, "Oh God, it was horrible!
What if it put venom in me?"

Jeff watched the color drain from her face as
she spoke her fears out loud. She needed to calm
down—being irrational posed more danger than the
suspected venom. "Let's warm you up by the fire
and I'll take a look around," he murmured in a
soothing voice, leading her by the waist.

"You don't believe me, but it was huge. Way
too big for a tarantula."

He propped Morgan up in the arm chair near the
fire and used the quilt to cover her body, and
then he kissed her forehead and returned to the
bathroom. Inside the tiny room he picked up the
glass, keeping his eyes peeled for any unwanted
intruders. Jeff knew that Morgan had a touch
of arachnophobia, and a seven-inch tarantula,
including leg span, would probably send her into
a tizzy—especially if she surprised the spider
and it defended itself.

A smaller part of him, however, feared that
Morgan was right and she had actually been attacked
by an animal—a tiny raccoon or squirrel. If so,

it was crucial to find the animal and make sure it did not have rabies. He threw the last of the glass into the trash can and hoped that when he returned, Morgan would be calm enough to explain what really happened, and could give him a better description of the creature.

As he was about to leave the room, a shadow moved behind the ceramic base of the toilet, catching his eye. Jeff cautiously took the small waste basket in his hand, hoping to trap the animal without getting bit. Rabies shots were painful and often caused side effects as miserable as the disease—if he could catch the animal, be may be able to spare Morgan the procedure.

$$***$$

Back on the chair, Morgan calmed her nerves through deep breathing exercises. The culprit had not been a spider—similar looking, perhaps—but definitely something else. Everything happened too fast for her mind to interpret what she had seen. If the animal had been rabid, she would need to see a doctor immediately. She felt drained of energy and wanted to sleep, but she had to stay alert so Jeff could take her to the hospital.

Morgan fought the lethargic wave creeping through her body as Jeff slowly entered the room.

"Did you find it?" she asked, her voice weak.

"Yeah," Jeff responded emotionlessly.

"Well, what is it?"

"Relax. It was a raccoon. Just as I thought."

Morgan was relieved that it was a raccoon, and not a strange, venomous creature, but was aware that the real threat of rabies loomed.

"Did you catch it?" she asked hopefully.

"No. I chased it through the bedroom and it got out the window." He continued to stare at her with no real expression.

Morgan hung her head.

"Don't worry, babe," he knelt beside the chair. "I'll take you to the doctor as soon as we get back, and you'll get the shots, just to be on the safe side. I'll take time off from work and stay with you the whole time."

Her eyes welled up with tears. "Take me home, please."

"I can't do that, not tonight. Trying to navigate the narrow, windy paths without light is dangerous. If I make a mistake, the car could get stuck or slide down an embankment." He stood up and moved towards the fire. "Then we'd have to hike out in total darkness, or wait till morning."

Morgan knew he was right, but the thought of having to wait until daybreak to see if she was infected made her nauseous. "Tomorrow then," she smiled, trying to be brave.

"Why cut the trip short," Jeff started. "Let's spend the next two days like we planned and then we'll see the doctor as soon as we get back. After all, we know it's just a raccoon."

"What?" Morgan could not believe what she was hearing.

"The incubation period is 10 days up to a whole year for rabies. And that's if you really *did* get drool in your mouth. You have nothing to worry about. We have plenty of time to start the treatment, so let's enjoy the weekend." He smiled. "Now how about I fix you something to eat?"

Morgan stared at her husband in disbelief. Sure, he knew all about the disease and could look at it scientifically, but when it was possibly affecting his own wife, she expected to see a little more concern. "I hope you're not being serious, because if you are I'm gonna need that whole bottle of champagne just to digest what you're saying."

"No," he quickly lifted the bottle from the coffee table in front of her and walked it to the kitchen. "Someone in your condition should not be drinking alcohol."

"I thought rabies were no big deal," she replied sarcastically. Her stomach churned loudly and she clutched at her belly.

"You're okay," he said as returned to her side.

Morgan bent over and heaved dryly. She swallowed and looked up, "My stomach is killing me. I feel nauseous."

Jeff stoked her neck, "I'll get you some water." He returned to the kitchen.

"Bring me a bucket or towel. I think I need to throw up."

"That's not a good idea," he said flatly.

"Damn it, Jeff! I don't know what has gotten into you, but you're acting like an asshole. Telling me there's plenty of incubation time and other pointless shit like some rabies documentary. *Might as well stay the weekend!"* she scoffed, imitating his callousness from earlier. "I'm your wife and you're acting like you don't care if I live or die!"

"That's not true at all," he protested, but remained monotone. "I need you to live."

She ignored him while the knotting of her stomach became unbearable. Morgan stuck her finger down her throat, hoping to induce vomiting. She did not know if that was the right action to take, but she felt something gross inside of her, and thought that if it came out, she would feel

better.   She wretched dryly and only managed to
spit out saliva.

"What are you doing?" Jeff actually raised his
voice, and ran to the chair pulling her hand away
from her mouth.

"Maybe I did get some toxin or something down
my throat.   I think puking it up will make me
feel better." Tears were rolling down her cheeks
from her efforts. "I've never done this before,
but I think all I have to do is push harder."
She raised her finger again, praying that success
would alleviate the pain.

"No!" Jeff restrained her hand.

"Jeff, what are you doing?" Her tear soaked
face pleaded with his cold stare.   His actions
made no sense to her. If he could not safely get
her to a doctor tonight, then she was willing to
try anything that might ease her suffering.

Jeff, however, thwarted her every move.

She broke his hold, "I need to try. Why can't
you help? Something is wrong with me, can't you
see that!" She returned her finger to her throat.

Jeff went into a panic. His stiff movements
from earlier vanished and his head twisted back
and forth between the room and his gagging wife.
He leapt toward the fireplace and grabbed the
hatchet off the wall.   In a swift motion, he
pulled Morgan's hand from her throat before any
vomit was extracted, and slammed it against the
wooden armrest.

"Jeff?"

Still holding her forearm tightly, Jeff brought
the hatchet down as hard as he could into her
wrist. Morgan let out a blood curdling scream as
the blade sunk deep into her flesh. Bone cracked
and tendons severed, blood spraying from the
initial contact.

Morgan stared in terror at her axe-wielding husband whose face was splattered with droplets of her own blood. The blade was a little more than halfway through her wrist, and it took some force for Jeff to pull the hatchet back up through the lacerated anatomy. When the blade finally exited her flesh, it left with a sickening squish.

Jeff's lifeless eyes did not even blink as he brought the weapon up above his head for another attack. Bloodied flesh hung from the sharp edge as it followed the same course into Morgan's mangled body. The second blow separated the hand from the arm, the disembodied appendage falling to the floor and rolling twice, smearing thick blood across the white carpet.

Emotionless, Jeff snatched a partially burnt log by its uncharred side and knocked it against the brick fireplace, causing the fiery end to fall off, leaving behind bright red embers. In less than two seconds the burning embers were pressed against the bloody stump, cauterizing the sliced ulnar and radial arteries. A helpless Morgan watched speechless, her body convulsing violently with fear and shock at the unprecedented event.

Jeff dropped the burnt log back into the fireplace and stared at his wife. "Sorry honey, but I didn't know what else to do."

Morgan finally found her voice, and let out a series of short, high pitched screams. Jeff tried to speak over her, "I couldn't let you do it." Morgan's shrill screams intensified when she caught sight of her hacked off hand lying on the ground. Her sobs grew uncontrollable, and she began to choke, unable to emit further howls.

"Now if you could just listen to me, we can put this behind us."

"W..w..why?" Morgan stuttered, trying to understand what caused her husband go insane.

Jeff walked past her and Morgan craned her neck to watch him as he entered the kitchen. The cabin was dark except for the fire and moonlight, but despite the poor lighting, Morgan could see dark patches covering Jeff's neck and the top part of his white shirt. He filled up a glass of water and returned, placing the cool glass in her left hand. Morgan refused to look down at the glass. Instead she kept her gaze near the low ceiling, knowing that seeing her burnt and disfigured body would throw her into hysterics again.

She breathed deeply, hoping to calm her nerves once again, but doubted it would ever work. "Why… why," it was the only word she could manage to get out.

Jeff made no response as a hissing noise emerged from all around them. Morgan's head circled, trying to pinpoint the source of the noise. Shadows moved across the cabin's walls, from the flames of the dwindling fire, distorting her view. Amidst the dancing shadows, she saw objects moving—from high corners, behind sinks, and near the floorboards, large dark shapes appeared and crept towards the couple.

Morgan recognized them as the same type of creature that attacked her earlier. As they drew closer, Morgan saw that each creature had a blackish-brown body the size of a human fist. They moved on thick legs that extended from either side of their circular body, holding them above the ground, and propelling them like slow moving crabs.

Jeff stood motionless as six of the creatures advanced. They were close enough for Morgan to see that their head and eyes *were* similar to that of a tarantula, but the two large pincers they sported on the sides of their mouth were much

larger than anything found on a spider. Morgan
wanted nothing more than to jump to her feet and
run, but she was too shocked and sickened to move
from the chair.

The largest of the creatures scurried past
Morgan's feet and up to her severed hand. The
oversized crab-spider hybrid let loose another
hissing noise and took hold of Morgan's dead
fingers with his two pincers. Horrified, she
watched the animal drag her lost limb across the
floor, back towards the kitchen. The remaining
creatures replied with a similar hiss that sent
shivers up Morgan's spine, then withdrew back
into their dark hiding places within the cabins'
walls.

Jeff stood with his back to Morgan, watching
their retreat. Now that he was closer to the fire,
Morgan could tell that the dark stain on his
shirt was blood. She leaned forward, trying to
get a better look, without causing him to turn
around. There were two puncture wounds on the
back of his neck responsible for the blood. It
looked like something was inside the bite marks.

Jeff turned around. "They seemed very pleased."

"Jeff," Morgan spoke very calmly. If they were
going to live through this, she had to ignore the
pain and disbelief she was experiencing. "You
have been bitten by one of those animals. I
think they might be poisonous, so why don't you
come over here and let me look at your neck."

Jeff made no attempt to move, just stared at
her.

"I think you are a little confused because
of the venom. That can happen. Please look
at me. Fight the venom. We need to leave here
and we're gonna need your help." She prayed
that her words were reaching him. The creatures
inhabiting their cabin were unlike anything she

had ever seen. She doubted that even Jeff, in all his nerdy insect wisdom, had come across a species such as these. Obviously, the bite and venom had the ability to confuse and disorient victims and must have injected something at the base of his neck.

Jeff walked towards her as if he was finally understanding, when more hissing rang out from within the walls. The hiss was at a much higher frequency then before, resembling a shriek.

Jeff stopped and went erect.

"Jeff, baby, please!" Morgan ignored the pain welling up inside the pit of her stomach. It felt like she was digesting broken glass.

"They need you," Jeff said and moved towards her again.

"Nooo!" Morgan screamed when she saw the fire reflect off the steel hatched he gripped in his hands. She kicked out her legs, but they were tangled in the quilt, making the blow to his shin ineffective. She kicked off the blanket and landed her foot into Jeff's crotch, bringing him to his knees with a groan of pain.

Morgan struggled to her feet, dizzy and queasy, and tried to get past him. She tripped on the quilt bunched at her feet and tumbled to the floor. She attempted to break her fall by putting out her hands, realizing too late she only had one left. When the ground contacted her tender and exposed stump, she screamed and writhed in pain on the carpet next to the fire.

Jeff regained himself and seized her moment of weakness by rolling her onto her back and pinning her to the ground. Sitting on her legs, Jeff brought her left arm above her head and held it tightly against the carpet.

"Jeff," she said in a soft tone, hoping to reach him, "I love you. What are you doing?"

He responded with a quick chop of the hatchet, the searing pain radiating from her rest up through the rest of her body. The carpet did not provide a solid cutting block, resulting in a laceration barely penetrating the carpal ligaments.

Jack hacked at the limb in a frenzy, missing his mark several times. Morgan slipped into blackness when the hand finally detached from her wrist.

***

Her eyes opened she saw Jeff sitting pensively in front of the fire. His head was down, and he did not know she was awake. She noticed that night was fading away, and an eerie pre-dawn haze penetrated the gloomy cabin.

It was a dream. A horrible nightmare. I fell in the shower and he's been watching over me ever since.

She thought she heard Jeff speak softly, but she did not see his lips move. The noise continued and grew louder, but Jeff was not the speaker.

I know that sound.

"No," she cried, getting Jeff's attention.

"We were so worried we lost you." He walked over to her. "Blood loss can take a person fast, but I felt confident I did a good job."

Her senses returned fully, and with it came the pain. Not sharp and piercing like earlier, but dull, throbbing spasms throughout her body. Morgan looked around, feeling paralyzed below her neck. She could no longer bear to look at or speak to Jeff, the sight of him repulsed her. She hung her head and received a horrific surprise—her mind was so overloaded that it was unable to make fast connections between what she saw and its meaning.

She saw a rope securing her to a chair, and on the ground were at least ten creatures greedily feasting on human flesh. Morgan saw her right hand, picked clean to the bone, with one crab-spider attempting to find a few last shreds of sustenance.

Her left hand, still rich with meat, sat in between two more of the monstrosities. One foot was eaten away except for pink nail polish across its toes, and the other foot, much fresher, just getting started on. The two biggest crab-spiders were in a corner working on what looked like an arm.

Jeff stood watching the smorgasbord as if he saw this sort of thing all the time. His glazed over expression belonged to some kind of monster—his body was merely a shell.

To keep her mind off the pain, Morgan thought back to their hike through the woods and remembered Jeff's comment about the wasp. *They use mind control, venom or secretions…scientists don't know exactly how it works…happens a lot in nature.*

Wasn't that what this was? Mind control. Jeff loved animals, but not enough to kill his wife for them. Perhaps getting bitten might have been better than being attacked and drooled on. *Which fate was worse? Dismembering your lover, or being dismembered?*

Morgan doubted there would ever be a Discovery special on this unique animal, whatever it was. Its venom was strong enough to control humans, an impressive feat. *Too bad Jeff is their slave. He would have been fascinated by the creatures.* Morgan chuckled at the irony despite the pain.

The word *slave* kept thoughts of the wasp and caterpillar's relationship in Morgan's head, and she realized in horror that Jeff was not being forced to kill her—she was being used as food, but she was being kept alive.

"Oh God!" she breathed as her blood-depraved mind made the last connection.

It did spit something into my mouth!

Searing pain exploded inside her stomach. She tried to scream but could only choke on blood that bubbled up into her esophagus. Underneath her bathrobe, her pulsating stomach tore open, revealing tiny pincers searching for air. The folds of her bloody wrap separated, and miniature crab-spiders crawled out from their bloody womb.

Jeff watched four babies exit his dead wife's eviscerated bowels to join their family. Like the poor caterpillar, Jeff's job was done. He protected the womb, and fed the kin. The venom released him and Jeff expired, falling to the floor, no longer useful—except as food.

About the author:

Jack Burton resides in Arizona where he practices his passion for teaching, heavy metal, and of course, horror. His short story "The Gambler" can be found in the horror anthology *Bonded by Blood II* available in January 2010.

Lisa Gurney

Buried Amidst the Butter Beans
An A-Z Story of Revenge

Alice drives home by rote, thinking about her night with Bobby; easy and safe as a Sunday afternoon and enough love to fill a cornfield—mirror-opposite from every other night she spends with her husband, Clyde. Bobby was not at work today, and she missed the note and piece of lemon candy he always leaves in her locker at Lorrey's Pesticide Plant where they both work.

Clyde's truck is in the driveway as Alice nears their yellow clapboard house, three hours earlier than expected from his trip up North, and thoughts of Bobby fly from her head like startled angels at the sight of him shoveling near her vegetable garden. Dirt from the unpaved road rises like creamy mist as she slows to a stop, her skin prickling with apprehension; Clyde is like clockwork—up at 5:45 am expecting his coffee hot and sugary before heading off to his job at old Grossman's farm, and home by 6 pm where he "'spects supper ready n' waitin' or there'll be hell to pay." Even-stepped, though her heart was tripping like a toddler in heels, she walks toward Clyde, noticing his shirt plastered to his back with grimy sweat, the front looking as if painted with her Big Boys, all red and pulpy.

Frightened now and barely breathing, Alice asks in a whisper, "Clyde, what are you doing home so early?"

Giving the hole he is filling one more shovelful of black earth before turning to look at her, Clyde says with a grin, "Why, just buryin' Bobby, honey."

He wipes his forehead with his arm, then rests it languorously on the shovel handle and says, "Killin' him was fun for me, but Alice, your pretty boyfriend here pleaded and cried like a baby with diaper rash."

"I tell ya darlin'," he goes on, "nothin' like fresh churned soil to bury an adulterer in…covers up real nice like God intended."

Just as her eyes glance down against her will into the almost covered pit, she catches the glint of something shiny to the left of it…*the watch, Bobby's watch, the one I gave him for Christmas*, and as if she has been hit in the stomach with a bowling ball, Alice sucks in air and crumbles to her knees moaning, sending Clyde dancing and cackling around the rows of butter beans. *Killed him…he killed my Bobby*, Alice repeats, eyes wide and disbelieving like a small child who's just been smacked for the first time by its mother.

Lit with an anger that forces her back to her feet, she lunges for Clyde's face with fingers bent claw-like and rages in a cracked voice, "You son of a bitch!"

Maneuvering gracefully for someone so laden with meanness, Clyde easily wards off Alice and grabs her by the hair from behind, forcing her back into the newly churned grave of her Bobby.

"Now you listen here you no good whore; consider yourself lucky you ain't lyin' beside ole' Bobby and that I'm lettin' you breathe another day," Clyde says, releasing her with a push, then spitting and turning his back, not the least bit troubled by the possibility of another attack from Alice.

On her hands and knees and still sputtering, Alice glances at Bobby's watch and just before her hand can close over it, Clyde's old farming boot meets her ribs and with a tiny thunder-like crack sends her off to the left of Bobby's grave.

'*Please, Lord, let him kill me too*,' she thinks, lying there between piercing breaths until she remembers Bobby's smile, a smile that would light up heaven, and her heart grows arctic with deadly thoughts.

Quietly, she gets up and limps to the house, listening to Clyde hum as he starts to shovel again. Red dots of pain dance in front of her. She cradles her ribs and climbs the back stairs to the kitchen.

Taking an old stained bowl from the cabinet, she shuffles over to the pantry. Under the lower right shelf, just behind neat stacks of jarred okra and covered by her Mama's hand-laced napkins, are two small packets she's been patiently storing for the moment when Clyde's meanness would grab hold of her and send her crazy. Voices of her Mama warning her away from Clyde ("that man ain't nothin' but trouble lookin' for a place to land,") keep her company as she beats eggs with the packets' contents. Working at the pesticide plant helped her get just the right ingredients for this special supper, one long in coming, and just a day overdone.

Xanthan Gum—to prevent the poison from creaming up—is the next ingredient she adds. "You'll never taste it you bastard, but you sure will feel it," she whispers as she starts to slice his favorite vegetable, picked from her garden that morning and toasty warm from the windowsill. 'Zucchini and cyanide for your supper tonight,' she says and smiles, 'and later, a nice cozy bed beside Bobby and the butter beans.'

Author's Note:

If you aren't familiar with A-Z stories, they contain 27 lines, each beginning with the alphabet in order (i.e., first sentence begins with A, second begins with B, and so on). Hence, these stories tend to bend the rules of structure, but only slightly!

About the author:

In 2007, Lisa Gurney quit her Fortune 500 job to pursue her dream of writing. Since then, her fiction and essays have been published both in print and online in the United States and Canada. She is the recipient of the 2007 National PRNDI Award for Commentary for her essay "A Witness to Violence." Lisa resides in Worcester, MA and welcomes comments at lisajgurney@gmail.com.

Jerry Enni

On a Lonely Stretch of Road

"Do you think we've gone forty miles yet?" Cally asked.

Dennis kept his grip on the steering wheel, but lifted his arm so he could look at the mileage below the speedometer.

"Pretty damn close, I'd say."

The remnant fiery glow of the setting sun bled out above the mountains to the west and bathed the alfalfa fields in a warm shadowy light.

Cally started chewing her lower lip.

"You want me to turn around?" Dennis said.

"No…I don't know. This says Patterson road. We're supposed to be on Yosemite until we hit 132. Says right here forty miles."

"Probably coming right up," Dennis said.

"Where the hell did Patterson come from. We're not supposed to be on…"

"Could just be one of those roads that change. Like back home, where Airport turns into West Lane when you get past Harding, then changes back to Airport way south. You know?"

"I guess," Cally said. "Call Jon, and see if they came this way, too."

Dennis pulled out his phone and the screen read: SEARCHING SVC.

"No service out here," he said and looked over to Cally, whose face was rife with worry lines. "Hey, come on, we'll be fine. Another half hour and we'll be there."

"Yeah," Cally said, and then rubbed the swell of her belly, "and I'll have to set up our tent in the dark."

Dennis looked down at her stomach. "I'll help you set it up. We'll get the headlights on our camp-spot. You getting movement?"

Cally rubbed her belly again. "Butterfly flutters."

"Give it a few more months and she'll be kicking you in the ribs. Remember what it was like with Evan?" Dennis asked, and then looked down at their son who was asleep in his booster seat between them.

Cally looked down too. "Yeah, I remember," she said and rubbed her belly again.

Dennis reached across Evan to place his hand on her stomach, and then she screamed.

"Jesus, watch out!"

He had his hands on the wheel and swerved just in time to miss two girls standing in the road. In the flash of his headlights he noticed a realty sign in front of the property behind them: FOR SALE – CHERRY ORCHARD – CASH CROP – 402-555-0984. He hit something—something big—because the whole back end of the truck went briefly airborne when the rear wheels went over it.

He stepped on the brakes and pinned the wheel to the right, trying to keep out of the irrigation ditch that preceded a high cornfield on the wrong side of the road.

The truck shuddered, a loud snap rang out, and they skidded to a stop just short of the stagnant shallow water of the irrigation ditch.

"Are you okay?" Dennis asked.

Cally scooted in her seat, adjusting her position. "I think so." She squinted her eyes tightly. "What about Evan?"

Dennis looked at his son. "Still sleeping,"
he said and put his hand on Evan's chest and felt
the rise and fall of his breathing.

Cally opened her eyes, and though she was
cramping and worried about the baby she carried,
she could not help the smile that crept across
her face. Evan was always one heavy sleeper.

Dennis undid his safety belt. "I better go
back and see what I hit."

"No!" Cally said.

He had the door opened and was about to jump
out onto the dusty shoulder. "What?"

"I don't like this," she said.

She looked down the road ahead of them. It
seemed to go on forever. Then she craned her
neck and looked back down the road behind them—
the same thing there, it just went on and on and
on. The leftover glow of the sun was nearly gone
and a translucent sliver of moon hung in the sky.

Dennis jumped out and was hit with the smells
immediately—the sweet repugnant smell of cow
shit, the fresh smell of cool water in the heat,
the earthy smell of mud, and above all else, the
smell of decomposition. Something, or maybe
some*things*, had died out here recently.

"Don't go back there, Dennis Thompson."

He looked up at her, perturbed. Then he looked
down where he heard a slight hiss.

"Shit!"

The front driver-side tire was flat.

"What?" Cally asked.

"Tire's gone."

"Can you put on a spare?"

"I could if I had a spare."

"Oh my god, Dennis. You took us all the way
out here and you don't have a stupid spare on the
truck? What's wrong with you?"

Dennis ran his hand through his hair and took a deep breath.

"Somebody cut it," he said in a very low voice.

"What!"

"Somebody cut the goddamn chain and stole it. I was gonna get another one when I…"

"What are you looking at, what is it?" Cally demanded.

"Wait here—somebody's coming."

In the dim light behind the truck, near an old shed that looked like it was one stiff breeze away from collapsing, Dennis saw two figures advancing toward the truck.

He started toward them.

"Dennis?" Cally called.

"Wait in the truck," he said.

Five yards down the road he looked back to his truck, worried about leaving his family, but eager to keep them in the safety of the vehicle.

They shined a light in his eyes and he could not see them very well. Two girls, about the same age, probably sisters because they sounded exactly alike. The first thing they said to him after shining the light in his eyes was: "Mister, have you seen our dog?"

Dennis tilted his head down and raised his hand to shield his eyes. "No, sorry, girls. I haven't seen any dogs. Afraid I might have hit something back there."

He could not see their faces, but he did make out the hems of their skirts. They were white once, but now were browned and yellowed with age. The girls did not wear stockings, either, and they both had knobby knees and worn out dusty black dress shoes.

The girls giggled then and dropped their flashlight. They ran snickering back down the road, past the shed and beyond.

"Hey," Dennis called out, but they did not stop. "Hey."

He picked up the light and followed the truck's skid marks. He wanted to see just what he hit.

Another fifteen yards down the road, right in front of the FOR SALE sign, he found the casualty. A large roll of old carpet stretched out across the two lane road.

"What the…?"

There was a flash of light in the woods and he decided he would drive on the busted tire. If he had to buy a new rim when he got back, then so be it.

A loud yelping bark came from the darkness that lay beyond the FOR SALE sign, and Dennis could see something moving there.

"Jesus, screw this," he said and turned to run back to the truck.

The beam of the flashlight returned, running up the length of the sisters' eerie faces.

"Mister, have you seen our dog?"

They looked at each other, and then looked up at Dennis.

He shook his head.

"Thomas," one of the girls said, "I think he's lying. I think he ran over old Grady."

In the light he could tell they were twins, maybe nine or ten, and they were not regular. The one on the left had her right eye poked out, and the one on the right had her left eye poked out. *Poked out*—there really was not any other way of putting it. The eye and everything else was gone, leaving a dark, hollow socket.

The way they moved made it seem like they were coordinating—they stepped in sync, turned on a dime, like they each drew the vision they missed from their own dead eye from the opposite living one of their twin.

"Promise, I do believe you're right. I think we should go and tell Papa."

"I didn't hit any dog! Look," Dennis said and shone the light down on the carpet. Only it was not a carpet anymore—now there was big bull mastiff lying with blood running from its mouth.

Dennis dropped the light and ran for his truck, glad he left the key in the ignition at the start position. If he had not, the tail lights would not have shined, and he would have been running blind.

"Cally, start the truck!" he yelled. He figured he could get away with 35-40 miles an hour on the rim. With that, if they were indeed on the right track, they would be in camp in less than half an hour—anything to get the hell out of there now.

He arrived at the truck and jumped in.

"Jesus, I said start the truck."

He turned the key and the headlights illuminated the scene before him.

Four men in pink bathrobes stood at the head of the truck. Another was at the passenger door with his hand on Cally's belly. Evan, thank God, was still buckled into his booster seat.

Dennis swung his fist at the man that touched Calley, and the man retreated. Then he stomped on the gas, the tires spinning in the dirt. The men in pink robes stepped aside as the truck dug in and took off down the road.

A minute later the whole tire shredded off the rim, the sound shrill and sharp in the empty night. Dennis saw a stream of sparks spewing off his left rim every time they hit a turn.

When the road sign showed that they were once again on Yosemite, they both relaxed a little.

They pulled into their campsite and Jon, waving his arms in mock exasperation and welcome, guided them into their parking spot.

Cally was rubbing at her belly again.

"You okay," Dennis asked.

She shook her head.

"Let me see," Dennis said, and raised her shirt.

Her tanned belly was smooth and opulent, except for a few small pale markings near her belly button. They sort of resembled a dog's paw, or a sloppily placed gnarled human hand.

Jon had a campfire going and there was food on the grill.

Dennis helped her out of the car and set up their tent, then carried Evan inside and laid him on his pad. Cally was already there.

"I'm sorry," Dennis said.

"For what?" Cally said.

He shrugged his shoulders.

"I'll get a spare when we get home. Okay?"

"Okay."

About the author:

Jerry Enni lives in a small house in the center of the San Joaquin valley with his beautiful family. By day he makes signs, and by night he writes stories; one of which you'll find in this anthology. He hopes you enjoy reading it as much as he enjoyed writing it.

Christin Haws

Hillbilly Hunt

Jimmy eased the screen door closed and crept down the back steps into the heavy heat of the July night, his left hand sweating around the shotgun. There was no moon to light his way to the barn, and his flashlight was still crammed into the back pocket of his almost outgrown jeans, but his feet knew the path even if his eyes had trouble seeing it.

This trip to the barn didn't take Jimmy inside to do chores, but around the back of it to meet up with his older brother, Billy.

Jimmy was going on his first hillbilly hunt.

All his brothers had done it, and fifteen year old Billy was taking him tonight. Jimmy had been both looking forward to it and dreading it since he had turned eleven in March. Although his brothers had all gone on hillbilly hunts, Jimmy didn't know what he was doing. Well, he knew they were going to the woods and Mama would have a fit if she found out, but that was it. Billy just told him they were going and to bring the shotgun and a flashlight behind the barn at midnight. He refused to answer any questions. The last one Jimmy asked, Billy answered by slugging him hard enough to leave a bruise.

Billy took the flashlight from him, but didn't turn it on. Jimmy felt clammy despite the heat as he and Billy tramped through the cornfield behind the barn, heading to the woods in strict silence, only the cicadas allowed to make any noise, following one cornrow dead on so they wouldn't get lost in the dark. The stalks crowded them, slapped at them. Jimmy knew it was just corn, but his imagination couldn't be convinced.

A light or a voice in the yard would be sure to wake up their dad. He was on his feet, shotgun in hand and nose pressed to the warm glass if he heard a chicken cluck funny; he'd probably just start shooting if he saw a light or heard a voice. Dad fretted a lot about people getting on his land. But Jimmy didn't understand why they couldn't use the flashlight or talk in the cornfield. Dad couldn't hear them that far out, not from the house, and shoot them; or worse, catch them out of bed after midnight and give them an earful, a beating, and extra chores. And even from the upstairs bedroom, Dad wouldn't be able to see the light if they kept it low.

Maybe *they* could hear them and that's why they had to be quiet. But they'd only be able to see the light in the middle of the cornfield if they flew and they didn't fly. At least, Jimmy didn't think they could fly. Otherwise, he'd have seen one by now. Probably.

Billy stopped. It took a half second for Jimmy to realize it against the monsters in his mind. He stopped just short of plowing into his brother and listened hard. Above the buzz of the cicadas, he thought he heard something move somewhere a little way off, past the end of the cornfield.

"Coyote?"

Billy elbowed him so hard in the ribs that it knocked most of the air from his lungs and he nearly dropped the shotgun. He looked up, blinking the tears from his eyes. Jimmy couldn't

see his brother's face in the dark, didn't have
to see his face to know that Billy was looking
at him, hard and mean.

No talking, right.

At first, Jimmy wondered if this was just a
big joke his brothers were playing on him. Now,
hunched down in the dark, trying to stay still
and not wheeze against the pain in his ribs, that
tickling feeling in his gut telling him that his
brother was pulling one over on him bled right
out.

Just as the ache in Jimmy's ribs began to run
down to his legs, Billy started walking again.
Jimmy hurried after him and shifted the shotgun
from his left hand to his right, rubbing his
sweaty palm on his shirt. They stopped again at
the edge of the cornfield. Billy turned on the
flashlight and pushed Jimmy ahead of him. They
ran across a short stretch of grass and into the
woods.

The light did little more than show a few
trees. Billy followed Jimmy, his hand on Jimmy's
shoulder, shining the light past him. They moved
slowly, Jimmy letting his older brother steer
him. Twigs, leaves, and other brittle things
crunched under their shoes. The hum of cicadas
sounded louder in here, almost like an intense
vibration. When it stopped, Jimmy felt it more
than he heard it.

A low moan drifted though the trees, but
no leaves moved. Jimmy jerked to a stop, the
sickening noise echoing in his ears. It didn't
sound human or animal. It didn't sound real.

But it was.

Billy squeezed his shoulder. Jimmy shifted
the shotgun to both hands and looked around. He
held his breath.

The light went out.

Jimmy's scream caught in his throat and came out as a strange choking sound. Billy let go of him. Jimmy clutched the shotgun and tried not to shake. The flashlight rattled frantically and he heard Billy whimper.

A breeze drifted through the trees, ruffling leaves and cooling the sweat on Jimmy's skin, making him shiver. The wind carried the stench of something sweet and rotten, like chicken gone bad. The urge to gag was strong and the urge to cry was even stronger.

That sound, that sad, painful groan, grew around him. It moved.

Jimmy choked on a sob. His breath hitched in his throat and tears filled his eyes. He wanted to run, but his legs wouldn't go.

The light came back.

Gray, hanging skin, maggots, and jelly eyes looked at Jimmy and Jimmy stared back, both of their mouths hanging open.

"SHOOT IT! SHOOT IT IN THE HEAD!"

Somehow, Jimmy's finger pulled the trigger and the face disappeared in a spray of buckshot.

Jimmy's ears rang. Tears mixed with the sweat on his face. His eyes felt like they were going to pop right out of his head. Billy dragged him backwards, screaming at him to run. Jimmy fell, but hardly touched the ground before he was up and moving, branches smacking his face and grabbing at his arms.

Jimmy broke through the woods and ran past his brother into the cornfield. Billy caught up with him and grabbed him, making Jimmy cry out. Clamping one hand over Jimmy's mouth, Billy dragged him to the ground and held him there.

Above his panicked breathing, Jimmy heard the screen door squeak. The flashlight clicked off and darkness hid them. The cicadas started buzzing again.

Billy gave him a good shake and let him up. The two of them sat in the dirt between cornrows, panting and trying to be invisible. The image of that face shattering played over and over in Jimmy's mind until his eyes adjusted to the dark and the bare outline of his brother scared it away.

The screen door squeaked again.

"What was that?" Jimmy's voice was soft and shaky. He wiped sweat and tears from his face with the back of a dirty hand.

Billy stood up and looked at the house. Jimmy struggled to his feet, the shotgun dragging him down. His legs didn't want to work.

"What did I shoot?"

Billy shrugged. "They walk in the woods, like they're lost or something. Never seen them come out and I can't say how they got in. They just wander around in there, moaning. Shoot them in the head and they stop." He shrugged again. "Clevie says some folks gotta die twice."

They walked back to the house in silence and Jimmy eased the screen door shut.

About the author:

Christin Haws is a writer without a day job living in a small town in the middle of a cornfield. It's highly specialized work that you can read about on her blog at http://kikiwrites. livejournal.com.

Rex E. Morrison

Midnight

"So, are you a cat person, or a dog person?"
Why do people ask me these things? It's not the actual questions I mind, but that they are talking to me in the first place. Have we suddenly become a society where it is acceptable to enter a stranger's space and ask random questions? I don't know, so I casually shrug my shoulders and go back to avoiding all eye contact after giving some vague response about waiting for a species to pick me.

The questions *did* start the wheels turning in my mind.

What kind of person are you? Dog? Cat?

The only thing I knew for sure was that I was definitely not a people person. Who knows why? I blame it on growing up in rural Nebraska and being home-schooled. But when I look around, I'm certainly not unique in that aspect and I haven't noticed others being as uncomfortable in social situations as I am.

Initially, I figured I was a dog person. After all, I have never been particularly close to cats. Of course, I've never been particularly close to anything, or anyone. I grew up, however, with an allergy to cats, and I was raised by a single mother who was conscientious, if not suffocating, in her efforts to keep me protected from things that might adversely affect me. Thus, no pets, no junk food, no video games…and no friends. I wasn't very well prepared when I went off to college. But I remembered the lessons well, and I kept my distance.

Truth be told, I never had to keep much distance. It was as though I had some sort of neon stamp on my forehead flashing *Stay Away* and *Odd Loner* alternately. It didn't help that I lived off-campus alone in a basement apartment just a few blocks from most of my classes. I had plenty of neighbors. Like many old homes in the area, the one I lived in had been converted into college housing. There were four total, two main floor and two basement apartments. All had a private entrance so I didn't have to worry about bumping unexpectedly into any of the other tenants.

I lived in the back basement apartment. My connection with the world, a small window situated above my kitchen sink that looked out on an overgrown patch of ground framed in lilacs that had years before established dominancy over the rest of the back yard. At night, a modicum of light from the street light seeped through the tangled foliage to dimly illuminate what I liked to refer to as my "patio entrance." Still, it was that little window and the secluded area it opened upon which changed my life. If not for that portal, I would never have met Midnight.

Midnight has lived with me now for two weeks. I chose the name because my first real friend is a coal black cat with piercing emerald eyes. Oddly enough, my first encounter with Midnight was in broad daylight. I don't know that I was ready for the responsibility of another creature living with me, but I am learning. I make sure that at least once daily I cradle Midnight on my lap and stroke him, scratching behind the ears, because he seems to enjoy that the most.

Besides, just learning the value of friendship, because I do think of Midnight as my friend, I have also learned that there is responsibility that comes along with caring for another. Midnight had only lived with me a few days when I heard two of the guys from the upstairs apartment complain to each other of the smell. I don't really know if they were talking about Midnight or their apartment. I can detect the stench of stale beer and old cigarette butts emanating from their apartment when the breeze is just right. It seems their goal, instead of graduating college, is to keep Anheiser Busche from going bankrupt. They have parties every weekend, and from the sounds of it they have plenty of people who are willing to help them reach their objective. It doesn't bother me. It is their connection to the world. My connection is through Midnight.

I found quickly that there really is a difference in kitty litter. Instead of the store brand, I now use Arm and Hammer Cat Litter. *Love your cats, not their odor.* I conscientiously change the litter every three days. I can't take the chance that the stink my neighbors were talking about was Midnight. I'm really not supposed to have pets, so I'm careful to keep Midnight out of sight.

But I'm getting ahead of myself. While I have never felt as alive as I have during the last two weeks, it was three weeks earlier that I first met Midnight.

I was standing at the kitchen counter, staring out the window, when a sleek outline caught my attention. I couldn't pull my eyes away from the creature as it sunned itself outside my window. It stared back at me and seemed to ask, "Can you find any flaw in me? Can you find one reason for not loving me, or at least respecting me?" As

I stared into his eyes, all my own shortcomings flashed through my mind. I found myself wanting to reach out and touch the form lying just out of my reach, to feel his muscles ripple, to *know* the knowledge that shone on the cat's face.

As I moved to push the hinged window outward, the black form fled. I was not able to get close enough to establish an intimate relationship with the creature. In that short span of time, however, I had become his captive. I sat in my cage and blankly gazed out the window. I, who had never taken an interest in the species, wanted this feline to come back.

I wanted to connect.

I went to the store and picked up a small bag of dried cat food. After I returned home, I put a bit in a small pie tin, pushed it through the open window, and sat my offering at his alter. Was it enough? Would he return and grace me once more with his presence?

The next night, as I walked up the path to my apartment, I noticed a dark figure by my window. *Could it be? No, the chances are too great against it.* Yet, there sat the same cat that had stared at me so intently just the day before, the pan of food empty. At that moment I named him Midnight. Partly because of his black fur, and partly because I like the midnight hour. I knew he held secrets in the same way that the night holds truths that dissipate with the dawn.

Over the next few weeks, we came to an understanding. He would grace me with his presence as long as I remembered to continue the offerings. Just no touching. If I got too close, he would dart off. Midnight became more and more comfortable with me. If I arrived home late from studying, he would be waiting, pacing nervously back and forth in front of the window.

He wouldn't even run off when I pushed the window open so I could set the food pan out.

I eventually got to leaving the window open in the hopes that Midnight would decide he wanted to inside. I needed a stronger connection, but I didn't want to lose what we had.

It had to be his choice.

Midnight has lived with me now for two weeks. I don't know how long he'll be able to stay, but now I know that I can connect with others.

My life was changed forever the night I came home from an intense night of research at the library. I couldn't help myself from checking out what the dark form was laying by my window. I made my way through the shadows and knelt by the limp figure I found. It was a cat. It was Midnight. He had died trying to climb in the window to my apartment.

A tear came to my eye. He had made his decision, and he *chose* me. Why the window gave way at such a time, I'll never understand. He's mine now, though, and I will take good care of him.

He'll never run away again.

About the author:

Rex Morrison was born and raised in Valentine, Nebraska. While he has lived in a variety of locales such as Idaho, Florida, and Wisconsin, he currently resides in Mitchell, Nebraska and is employed during the school year as an English instructor. Summers are filled with camping, canoeing the Niobrara, connecting with friends, and finding an adventure or two locked away in the pages of a good book.

Lucas Pederson

Push

They say children haunt the railroad crossing.

Of course "they" might be off their medication.

I don't believe a word of it. It's just a stupid old town legend.

A bus full of school kids stalls on the railroad tracks. The train is moving much too fast, hurtling at them like a massive iron beast, the children stuck inside.

Crash.

Suffer the little children.

That's the story anyway, and it's complete bullshit. I have enough to worry about.

I speed over the railroad crossing where the accident supposedly took place without looking for a train.

Some say they've seen the ghosts of children wandering around the tracks, all red eyes and grinning teeth.

Demon children.

A shiver trickles down my spine.

A mile or so from the tracks, my car begins to make a shrill squealing noise, but I continue driving. A few minutes later, the squealing stops.

Grandpa says there's something wrong with the alternator and I need to get it checked out.

Problem one is I can't afford to have a mechanic look at it. Burger King pays for gas and the car payment, and that's about it.

Problem two is my dad won't cough up the money I need to buy a new alternator.

Grandpa says it will hold up for maybe another week, but not much longer.

My car is my escape, and I need it to get away. Without it, I'll be stuck with them, and maybe even wind up like them. Crazy.

There's a gravel road ahead on the right.

My hands tighten on the steering wheel.

Here we go.

***

I pull into the driveway and there's Sid, naked and running around the overgrown lawn, arms waving, mouth wide open.

"Damn it," I growl and skid to a stop in front of the garage.

I turn the car off, grab my Burger King uniform, and get out. I can hear Sid's wails.

The sun is a hot fire on my fair skin. Late July is a bitch for me, my most hated part of the summer season.

Sid's wailing approaches.

He's on the other side of the car, slapping the hood and making loud whooping noises. His blue eyes are wide, wild and shifty.

He's ten years old and has Dissociative Identity Disorder. Or in other words, he has a multiple personalities. There are two other boys that live in Sid's mind, and both are hideous brats and utterly insane.

The thing slapping my hood is not Sid. He's someone, or something, else named Burn. The other entity, Ty, isn't as feral. Ty never wails and he never pounds on my hood, either. Ty rarely ever comes out at all.

I note a thick brownish substance on Burn's hands. It splatters all over my hood with each methodical slap. More of the brownish stuff smears his forehead, neck and chest.

Something nudges my leg. Absently, I reach down and scratch behind one of Missy's floppy ears. She's a Springer Spaniel, and perhaps my only true friend in the world. She licks my hand and I start around the car.

It occurs to me what that brownish substance is about half past the front bumper.

Shit.

I stop and glance around.

Either mom is asleep (I can't imagine how with all the noise Sid makes) or she forgot to take her pills.

I figure for the latter.

Burn clamors onto the hood of my car and jumps up and down, his shitty buttocks clenching and unclenching as he howls at the early afternoon sky.

I stare at him, thinking, *Mom forgot Sid's meds, too.*

My hands squeeze into taut fists, jagged fingernails biting into my palms.

Unlike the rest of my immediate family, I'm not on any meds, and there's nothing wrong with my brain. It seems strange, me being the only one, but that's how it is. And the strain of caring for them is taking its toll on my personal life, maybe even my sanity.

I resent them, but I love them, as if that makes sense.

My hands relax at my sides. Somewhere close a bird twitters while crickets chirp in the overgrown lawn.

I draw in a deep breath of manure-fragranced air and blow it all out slowly.

"Sid," I say. "Sid, get off my car."

Sid stops jumping and thrusts a reeking finger at me. "Wrong name! Wrong name!"

I sigh. "Okay, fine. Look, Burn, get off my damn car. Now."

Burn grins. He leaps off the car and goes screaming around the corner of the house.

I press my lips together, choking back the roar of irritation burning at the back of my throat like sizzling bile.

Why do I even bother? What good can I possibly be doing here?

I can't go shopping at the mall. I can't go to parties. And inviting friends over? Ha. Yeah, like that will ever happen. One look at my brother and they will run for the hills, shrieking in horror.

In short, I have no life.

I enter the house of madness.

* * *

Mom is on the couch, crying into her hands.

I go to her and take her hand in mine. She's trembling. She looks up and I start to cry, too.

When did she start looking so old?

"You forgot again, didn't you?" I say, already knowing the answer.

She sniffles, and her hand squeezes mine too hard.

Her sobbing face contorts. "Don't tell me what I forgot, you little bitch!"

I wrench my hand out of her grip.

She pitches forward, sobbing.

I step away, rubbing my hand with the other. Her words still have a way of shaking me. Her words hurt me the most. It's so hard to hear stuff like that spoken by your own mother, even when she can't help it.

Mom barks at the ceiling, a shrill yipping sound, and then buries her face in her hands again, her shoulders hitching with the sobs.

Mom has Tourette's syndrome.   It's getting worse.

Mom's right arm shoots out at me, her fingers wriggling in the air only an inch or two from my stomach.   Then she yanks it back, crying louder.

Tics.   The doctor calls them tics.

I catch a "sorry" amongst the harsh crying.

The doctor says she needs a higher dose of meds and a short time in the mental ward at the hospital to get things on track again, but Dad refuses to do any of it.

Personally, I think he's wrong. Mom is hurting. She's out of control, and she needs help, but Dad blows me off every time I mention it. He knows, and still he lets her suffer.

I go to the bathroom and come back with a glass of water and three pills.

A cocktail, I guess it's called.

It takes ten minutes to get her to eat the pills.

***

"Mom and me are goin' out t'night," Dad says. He pops a pill into his mouth and washes it down with a swig of Pepsi. Finishing the can, he belches loudly.

Dad is bi-polar, though it's not out of control and most times no one can guess he has it. He's good at hiding it from people.

"Out?" I say. "Didn't you hear what I said? She needs real help, Dad."

We're standing in the kitchen. I'm in front of the sink, the soggy remnants of Sid's morning cereal pooling in the drain. Dad closes the refrigerator door, another can of Pepsi in his large hand.

"Bull," he says and pops the top on the can. "She's getting plenty of good help here. I can't afford the bills. You know that. We've already been down this road, Emily."

"Dad..."

"That's enough. Let it go."

Sigh.

He walks out of the room without another word.

I gape after him, tears prickling my eyes.

"Hey, Em," Sid says and hurries into the kitchen.

I wipe at my eyes. "Oh. Hey. How you feeling?"

He pauses near the fridge. "Okay. Why?"

He only remembers some of what happens when one of the other personalities rise up and torment.

I shake my head. "Never mind. Mom and Dad are going out tonight."

"Cool," he says, and smiles. His eyes shift toward the open kitchen doorway. "Can we watch scary movies?"

I shrug. "I guess."

Sid jumps up and down and trots over to me. We hug. When Sid is himself, he's the greatest brother a big sister can have. I hug him tighter, close my eyes. Tears squeeze out from between my eyelids. After a time, he struggles free, grabs a can of Pepsi and tromps up the stairs to his bedroom.

The medication helps. It's not a cure, but it helps bring my brother back out of whatever void the other two throw him in when they decide to come out and play.

Missy nuzzles my thigh. I kneel down and hug her, and let her lick my hand. She's such a good dog.

She's like my sister, and I love her.

"C'mon, Missy girl," I whisper and ruffle her big, floppy ears.

Together, we go into the living room to watch some TV.

***

"Lock all the doors and windows when we leave," Dad told me before stepping outside. "All of them. Lock everything. Understand?"

I did, and told him so.

I close the front door and run the bolt home—*snick*—and go to every window, making sure each lock is secure. Most are.

I lock the back door, and remember the basement.

I clear my throat and step to the basement door. Sweat beads at my hairline, and the tiny hairs at the nape of my neck hackle.

A few seconds pass and I choke down my fear of a boogeyman. It's no time to be scared.

I open the door and flip on the light.

I stare down and shiver.

Before I know it, I'm in the basement and hurrying to the small windows, dragging along a small wooden step stool either Mom or Dad forgot down there.

One window is open, letting in a whiff of summer air.

Frown.

Why is this open?

I glance around the dim basement. My eyes spy the preserves my mom makes, then scan the dark hulk of the furnace and its cohort, the water heater. Cobwebs hang in ugly swags and tatters from the wooden ceiling.

I fix on a black square hole to the right of the furnace.

The crawl space.

I shake my head, stand on the step stool and slide the window shut.

It doesn't close.

It screeches to a halt an inch or two from the edge of the frame. I yank it back, and push again.

It sticks in the same spot.

Weird.

I shrug and slam the window as close as I can to the frame and call it good.

Mom and Dad will only be gone for a few hours.

No biggie.

I jump off the step stool and start across the basement when I hear a scuffing sound, like a boot shifting position on dirty cement.

I stop, my eyes darting to the utterly black crawl space.

I sprint to the stairs, race up them and slam the door behind me. I pull the bolt across and back away, my heart trip-hammering.

After a second or two I laugh at myself for being so stupid.

There's no one down there.

I turn away from the door and walk to the living room for the horror movie marathon.

***

Some marathon.

Sid gets halfway through a zombie flick and takes off for his room, screaming.

In knew this would happen. Sid talks big, but never delivers, which is fine. I stop the movie and go to Sid's room. His door is shut and I knock.

"Hey. It's just a movie, kiddo. It's not real. Can I come in?"

Sid takes a long time to reply. When he does, his voice is trembling. "Y—yes."

When I enter the room, my brother is on his bed, blankets wrapped around him.

I sit on the bed.

Missy jumps up beside me and licks my hand.

"You know it's not real, right? All fake."

"Z-zombies aren't real?"

I laugh. "Of course not. Do you think God would allow that to happen? Remember what Grandma said? God loves you and would never let anything hurt you."

"I—is God here now?"

I smile. "He's always around, you know that."

Sid slips his head out of the blankets. His eyes are wide, but the initial scare seems to be gone.

"No zombies?"

I nod. "No zombie, vampires, or werewolves. All fake."

Sid wants me to hold him for a little while. And before long, his trembling eases.

***

Later, Sid brushes his teeth and goes to bed.

I sit up and finish watching the zombie flick, Missy snoring away beside me on the couch.

Then I go to bed.

Missy snuggles in beside me and the next thing I know, I'm sleeping.

***

A sound wakes me.
I squint at the alarm clock.
2:32.
I groan, and close my eyes.
I reach out for Missy and she affectionately licks my hand.
Sleep.

***

Drip-drip, drip-drip…
Must have left the faucet on a little after brushing my teeth.
Squint at the clock.
3:30.
I reach out my hand for Missy and she licks it. I smile and drift back into sleep.

***

Drip, drip, drip, drip…
What the hell?
5:45.
Damn faucet.
I throw the blanket off and storm to the bathroom outside of my room, and flip on the light.
It takes me a moment to realize what I'm seeing. When I do, I scream and stumble away from the bathroom.
Missy hangs by a length of telephone cord from the shower curtain rod, cut sternum to groin, her guts in a lumpy, bloody mass on the floor.
The dripping noise was the sound of her blood falling into the tub and spattering on to the floor.
I whirl around and run for the phone in my bedroom.

How could she be dead if she was licking my hand?

I pick up the receiver and put it to my ear.

It's dead, and the cord is missing.

I see a note on my night stand.   It reads *humans can lick too.*

A low grunt startles me, and a tall, black silhouette stands in my doorway.

"So sweet," he whispers.

I scream as he enters the room, pick up the phone and throw it.

The phone strike the man in the head and he doubles over, growling.

Not a man. A killer.

Working up the courage, I bolt past the snarling man and slam the door behind me.

I reach Sid's room and throw open the door.

Splashed blood covers the entire room, even Sid's coloring books at the far end. I spot a small, pale hand on the pillow, shriek and run to the stairs.

Poor Sid.   Poor Missy.

I storm down the stairs, grab my keys from the holder and run outside.

From inside the house, I hear loud, ominous laughter.

My heart rapping in my chest cavity, I get into the car and start it.

I'm tearing down the driveway in reverse when I see a tall shadow run to my mom's old Cavalier.

"No," I gasp.

I keep thinking of Sid's room. All that blood. *Oh, my Sid.*

I think of Missy hanging there, guts all over the floor, blood soaking her fur, her blood staining the porcelain and tile.

I spin my car into the gravel road and hit the gas. The shrill squealing of the alternator sends my speeding heart into triple time.

Then it shrill noise quits and I'm racing to where gravel meets the black top.

I glance in the rearview mirror, and a pair of headlights flash at me.

"Shit, shit," I whine, skidding onto the pavement, taking a left, pressing the gas to the floor.

The headlights flash and taunt me.

He's gaining.

The killer punches the gas and cuts the distance between us in half.

He's so close now.

Crying, I see the railroad crossing ahead, the red lights are flashing.

A train is coming.

My speedometer's needle hovers just above ninety.

Then, the squealing returns, much louder and more threatening.

"No. Damn it! No!"

My car sputters and stalls about fifty years from the tracks, and I'm rolling freely, the car chasing me honking wildly.

My car slows, and rolls to a stop on the tracks. I look to my right, into the large bright light surging toward me.

Gasping, sobbing, I reach for the door handle, and freeze.

Sid is looking in at me. His face is solemn, his bright white eyes glittering.

"S-Sid?"

He nods, takes hold of my side mirror, and twists it.

Slow movement catches my eye.

FF-HONK, FF-HONK! The train blasted its horn.

I look in the mirror and can't believe what I'm seeing.

Children. Over a dozen of them.

Pale faces, dressed in tattered clothing, take a position near my car, placing their small hands on the rusting exterior.

The train is so close.

I glance in my rearview mirror, but instead the Cavalier, I see a smiling little girl in pigtails.

They're dead. They're ghosts. The kids from the bus acciden—

I turn to Sid. He nods at me, as if reading my mind.

Then, with a tremendous jerk that whips me in my seat, the dead children push my car away from the crossing. I glance in my rearview mirror, my breath catching in my throat as Mom's Cavalier bursts onto the crossing. Then I see nothing but fire.

The explosion rocks my car on its frame and sends it rolling a few more feet away. Shards of steel and burning plastic rain down over me.

The train's brakes screech.

Tack-tack.

I look out my window. Sid is smiling at me, glances up at the sky, nods, and looks back at me again.

He mouths the words: "I love you."

"I love you," I manage.

He smiles and then he's gone.

***

The next day, my mother and father wail while they take my brother's body parts out of the house.

I notice the tiny handprints in the dust on my car.

About the author:
Lucas is the author of over twelve short stories in various anthologies and e-zines, including his most recent in: Bards and Sages Quarterly, Blackness Within Anthology (edited by Gill Ainsworth of Apex Magazine), Mausoleum Memoirs Anthology (House of Horror), and Tooth Decay Anthology (Sonar 4). He lives humbly in northeast Iowa with his wife and their three daughters.

Coming Soon...

A horrifying anthology of terror on the high seas! It will scare you sea-ll-y!

Visit Pill Hill Press online at www. pillhillpress.com

Coming Soon...

He that sat on him was called Death, and Hades followed with him. And power was given to them over a fourth of the earth, and that they should kill with sword, and with hunger, and with death, and with the beasts of the earth… Revelation 6:8

A thrilling anthology of war, conquest, famine and death, with stories written by established masters and up-and-coming stars. Armageddon has never looked so good!

Visit Pill Hill Press online at www. pillhillpress.com

LaVergne, TN USA
04 May 2010
181548LV00002B/144/P

9 781593 306113